The Tarot Mysteries by Bevan Atkinson

The Emperor Card
The Empress Card
The High Priestess Card
The Magician Card
The Fool Card

THE HIGH PRIESTESS CARD

THE HIGH PRIESTESS

A Tarot Mystery

by

Bevan Atkinson

Electra Enterprises of San Francisco

ISBN 978-0-9969425-2-2

Acknowledgements

Thanks to my writing cheerleaders, especially my cousin Nancey Brackett, who motivates me every day to do the work. My sister Chris Hess is always willing to bring her unerring eye for detail to the details. Marc Sason was "honored" to be namesaked. Judi Cooper Martin was okay with being included as long as I didn't kill her, and, especially since she invariably encourages me to "keep going!" she remains alive and well in this work. Afrikahn Jahmal Dayvs is steadfastly the best sort of human being. Lana Flatt is the new friend you hope to make at some point in your life. David K. Nelson kindly provided excellent draft horse information. Thanks also to my beloved Kiki, Julia Rollit Shumway, who knows that her Percival will always adore her, and to Duane Unkefer for his manuscript expertise. Also for his perennially useful advice, even if communicating with him is like exchanging microfilm with a secret agent man. But he sends back the manuscript coated in chocolate, so okay.

For Jean Morrow Bevan
"One can pay back the loan of gold, but one dies
forever in debt to those who are kind."

Religion's for those who believe in hell and a spiritual belief is for those who've been there.
    – M.C. Beaton, *Death of an Addict*

And then there's America—a country, I understand, remarkably well-supplied with religions.
    – Dorothy L. Sayers, *Unnatural Death*

≈】≈

Fact: There is no such thing as a bad lemon bar. I have done the research.

I was embarked on such research lately because it had been some weeks since my last (mis)adventure with Thorne. Thorne's now-and-again day job is protecting people who require that sort of thing. I have, on a couple of occasions now, involved myself in the sideline of figuring out why the bodies needed to be guarded.

Thorne Ardall is a very tall person, six-foot-eight-ish, suntanned, with a mop of straight blond hair, and deep-set green eyes that glint with brown and yellow flecks. In terms of sheer mass, he is pretty much the human equivalent of the Great Wall of China.

We met when he crashed his car into my house one foggy night in San Francisco. He had been shot, and we joined forces to catch the murderer of his employer and attempted murderer of himself, after which Thorne moved into a modest but comfortable apartment on the ground floor of my home.

Yes, thank you, I know how absurd that must seem to normal humans. But I live in San Francisco, where normal humans need not seek residency.

He and I are housemates—well, more than that—but with my checkered romantic history I avoid elaborating and possibly jinxing our more-than-housemate status.

All that said, I can tell you there are certainly exceptionally outstanding lemon bars, such as the one I was now savoring, which triggered the requisite full salivary alert.

This particular lemon bar was purveyed by the East-West Café in Daly City, and it was ferrying supreme contentment to my mouth with every forkful. Across the top was a liberal lacing of dark chocolate sauce, an extra touch that is proprietor/chef Rose Sason's personalization, just for lucky me, of an already great dessert.

Rose understands and endorses my point of view about dark chocolate. Bless her.

Born in the Philippines, Rose enjoys amusing

the café's patrons with her hand-lettered daily menu. My dessert was listed as Lemmy-Chockety Bah. If you eat at the Café often enough, as I do since I do not cook unless forced to do so by food despots who should know better than to require it of me, you acquire a creative culinary vocabulary without—I thank the beneficent gods—acquiring any creative culinary skills.

I was enjoying my chocolate-slathered lemon bar without interference from Thorne, who knows better than to get between me and my dessert, even if at 260 pounds he is twice my size. Motivation trumps muscle-power is my credo when it comes to desserts.

I looked up when I heard the café door open because Thorne shifted his normally boulder-like position. He invariably sits with his back to the wall and an eye on all the exits.

DeLeon Davies, wearing his black working suit, white shirt, black cowboy boots and colorful tie, walked in and was headed over to our table.

DeLeon is the world's coolest human being. He is also my friend, and I am fortunate for that. Among other much more lucrative pursuits, he drives people around in his black Lincoln Town Car, "to stay in touch with my peeps," he says. I have availed myself of both his chauffeur services and encyclopedic knowledge many times during the years I have known him.

Thorne stood to greet DeLeon, and they ex-changed a complicated choreography of hand grips and shoulder bumps, minus any words. DeLeon is shorter than Thorne. At maybe six feet or so he is still a substantial presence, but unless one plays tight end for an NFL team, everybody is shorter and less substantial than Thorne.

I stood up to hug and kiss DeLeon because I believe one should take advantage of every op-portunity to hug and kiss handsome men.

DeLeon bore dark half-circles in the normally pecan-colored skin under his eyes. His wiry gray-ing hair was pulled back into a rubber band at his nape. He looked unsettled. This in itself was un-settling. The world's coolest human being does not let anything unsettle him, at least that I'd ever seen.

He pulled a chair over from an adjacent table and we all sat. I was about to ask him how he had tracked us down, but he is DeLeon and he knows exactly where I can be found at mealtime: some-place where someone else, preferably Rose Sason, prepares yummy vittles and then does the dishes afterward.

"Miz Xana, you on your feet again." Even un-settled, DeLeon extended the courtesy of noticing others first.

"Yes," I said.

I had broken my ankle into smithereens not

long ago, while helping Thorne figure out who was targeting his most recent personal security client. My nickname is based on Alexandra, which was too much for my baby sister to manage, so she dubbed me "Ex-Anna," and the nickname stuck.

"Long haul," DeLeon shook his head.

"It was."

"You good now?"

"I'm using the cane for the time being." I touched the handle that rested on the table edge. "It was three and a half months before I was allowed to put weight on all the bionicity, so it's taking me a minute to figure out the whole walking thing from scratch. But I'm doing great. Thanks for asking."

"I was worried."

"You helped me so much, DeLeon. You were an angel, and I won't ever forget it."

He patted my hand where it lay on the cane. Then we were all quiet. DeLeon turned and stared across the room, out the window at the traffic passing by on John Daly Boulevard.

He tapped his fingers on the wood-grain laminate tabletop.

He sighed.

I looked at Thorne. Thorne was watching DeLeon, seeing everything.

Thorne looked at me from under his thatch of

hair, his eyes expressive and his face immobile. He was telling me, as he tends to tell me with his prodigious economy of words, that it was my job to conduct the inquiry.

I set my fork down on the plate alongside the remainder of my lemon bar. It took massive self-discipline, but my friend DeLeon was unsettled, so I let go of the utensil that was ferrying lemmy-chockety contentment to me.

"DeLeon?"

He turned back to face me.

"My daughter."

"Which daughter?"

DeLeon had two daughters, the older one a married attorney and the younger one in high school. His son Terrell helped out with the chauf-feuring during the summer, when he wasn't at-tending industrial engineering classes at Stanford.

"My baby. Netta. They took my Netta."

DeLeon's voice filled up his throat and he choked on it as he spoke. Thorne sat forward and put his dinner-plate-sized hands flat on the table, ready to push himself up and go.

As Othello said, "Farewell the tranquil mind!"

"Do you know who has her?' I said.

"This cult run by some crazy woman."

"A woman is running a cult?"

"She callin' herself some Egyptian goddess name and sayin' all the people with her are her children. I looked her up. She say she 'Renenet, goddess incarnate of prosperity and abundance.'"

DeLeon can speak English like a Yale Honors Literature professor if he wants to. Right now he didn't want to.

"Netta is how old?" I asked.

"Just sixteen. She 'n her Momma been havin' some trouble 'bout Netta's boyfriend, and a month ago Netta took off in the middle of the night. We thought she went with this boy, but turns out no. So we been goin' crazy 'til today a friend 'a hers brought us a note from Netta sayin' what happened."

DeLeon turned to Thorne. "I couldn't think what to do 'til I thought of you."

DeLeon and Thorne were looking at each other in that meaningful way that men reserve for themselves—the look men use to say stuff, about the world and their troubles and their battle plans, without saying any actual words.

"How did she wind up in a cult?"

"This boyfriend we didn't like. She's sixteen. You know how that can be. He's twenty-five. I went to the cops, believe it or not, but it turns out there really ain't much they can do, even she's underage, if the girl wants to be with the man. This cop told me to make friends with him instead of tryin' to chase him off, and count on him or Netta gettin' tired of it."

"But so far nobody's gotten tired."

"Not so far. But she and Maxine had some big fuss a few weeks back. Maxine won't tell me what it was. Netta took money from Maxine's wallet and left a note said she was goin' on the bus to her Aunt Patricia's down in L.A. Her note to her friend just now says she went to Marysville instead."

"Is there a reason you don't just call the cops now that you know where she is? She's underage. Legally they can't keep her."

"That's gonna take too long. The po-po go and ask questions, knock on the door, let those people know they lookin' for Netta, give them time to do somethin'. I don't believe we want to give them time for that."

As DeLeon spoke his voice twisted into desperation. I took DeLeon's hand and squeezed it, shaking it a little the way you do to emphasize what you're saying.

"Okay. Don't you worry now. Thorne's going to go get her for you. Netta's going to come back home safe and sound."

I stood up to hug him goodbye. DeLeon's eyes were red and tears pooled at his lower lids when I hugged him.

"Wait," said Thorne in his deep rumble of a voice.

DeLeon and I looked at him. Thorne speaks so

seldom that one tends to swivel and stare.

"It's a cult. Not a simple extraction."

"What are you thinking?" I asked Thorne, sitting back down. DeLeon stayed on his feet.

"Weapons, suicides, dead-bolted entries and exits, underground chambers, dogs, kids."

"I figured all that," DeLeon said. "It's why I came to you instead of headin' up there on my own. But I have to get Netta out of there. Her note means she's ready to come home. She's countin' on me."

"We'll get her." I put my hand on his forearm. "You came to Thorne because you know he can do this without any harm coming to Netta. To anyone."

"I don't mind if whoever talked her into goin' up there gets harmed right into a hole in the ground."

"Can you arrange for that?" I said to Thorne.

Thorne's mouth turned up slightly at the corners. This is a toothy grin for him, and a definite affirmative.

Thorne stood, dropped money on the table, and strode quickly to the exit. DeLeon turned and followed.

"Where are we going?" I called out, slinging my purse over my shoulder, grabbing my cane with one hand and the last two bites of my lemon bar with the other, gimping as quickly as I could after them.

DeLeon heard the bump of my cane on the floor and, ever alert for the most courteous action to take, came back and held out his arm for me.

We heard Thorne shout *"Home!"* just before he slammed the door of his black BMW and started the engine.

The big Beemer's tires chirped as Thorne gunned it through the traffic signal at the corner and was gone. DeLeon and I went slowly down the steps to the café's parking lot. For now I have to go down steps like a toddler, my hand clamped in a death grip on the railing.

"The computers," I said to DeLeon, as he handed me into the Lincoln's back seat. "By the time we get to the house, he'll know what's what and he'll have a plan."

"Whatever that man says to do, that's exactly what I'm gonna do. That man is mighty mighty."

No argument there.

I ate the last two bites of lemon bar as DeLeon pulled out and headed west toward the ocean. The lemon bar was still excellent, but contentment was no longer the primary factor in the experience.

It was a lemon bar. By finishing it I was performing a sacred duty. I am confident everyone will understand.

≈2≈

The two dogs rushed to greet us as we walked into the house. Hawk, the black Great Dane/Mastiff mix, focused his attention on me. Kinsey, the brown Welsh terrier mix, aimed her plea for attention at DeLeon.

Foiled by our cursory greeting, they retreated to their round floor beds in the entryway alcove.

The two all-black housecats, Katana and Meeka, stayed curled up against each other on the ottoman in the living room. Katana may have raised an eyelid, but it was a mere peek if he did.

Upstairs, DeLeon and I walked into the computer room, where all the screens were lit up and the printers were spewing out paper.

The computer room had been, until Thorne set up shop by installing wide surfaces crammed with electronics, a seldom-used bedroom on the third floor of my house on 48th Avenue in San Francisco. From the side window we could look out at Sutro Park and the Pacific Ocean through the cypress, eucalyptus and Norfolk Island pine trees.

Maps, photographs, and newspaper articles were sliding out of the printers. Thorne held up a hand, signaling us to give him time.

"Would you like anything?" I asked DeLeon. "Tea? Water? Coffee?"

"How soon we leavin'?" he asked Thorne.

"An hour."

"Then I'm going to go get some provisions together," I said, heading for the kitchen downstairs on the second floor. San Franciscans almost always live one story up from street level in long, narrow houses perched atop a ground-floor garage.

Let me be clear: "Getting provisions together" does not count as cooking. No burners would be lit in the process.

"I'll make the coffee," offered DeLeon. This was not selfless voluntarism. DeLeon has tasted the coffee I make. I am a tea drinker, and I make splendid tea. Making tea involves boiling water and pouring the boiling water over dry tea leaves.

Boiling and pouring are the sort of cooking at which I can excel.

I assembled turkey sandwiches, some with avocado and lettuce and some with cheese and tomato. I added bacon to a couple of them because bacon is like dark chocolate: a universal bonus when layered onto just about any other food. I thought about it, and reopened one sandwich, slathered some cranberry sauce on it, and wondered why there is always a can of cranberry sauce available in the pantry.

Go check your pantry. You'll see.

The dogs trotted into the kitchen as soon as they heard the refrigerator door open. They planted themselves directly behind me, prepared to tag-team a high-low tripping effort should I turn around with food in my hand.

The cats ambled in at the sound of the can opener. Katana, the bigger of the two, jumped onto the counter and I promptly pushed him off again, our daily ritual. Meeka rubbed back and forth against Hawk, explaining as clearly as she could, cat-to-dog, that any food that came his way really belonged to her.

I realize my house is occupied by far too many pets for most people's taste. As my friend Yolanda once said about such people, "If they don't like it, there's no law requiring them to come over."

DeLeon poured coffee into a thermos and

screwed on the cap. I poured boiling water over Darjeeling tea bags in a pot, waited a couple of minutes, and poured the steeped tea into another thermos. I slid a dozen oatmeal raisin cookies into a bag and zipped it shut.

Standing at the counter, lowering the cooler's lid, I heard the inner voice that calls me "Child" tell me to fetch my tarot cards.

Uh-oh. But in another way, it was good news.

Mind in a minor muddle, I stood still, considered how much time it would take, and made the decision.

≈3≈

I am a tarot reader. I don't work out of a store-front with neon signs showing a mystic eye or the outlined palm of a hand, not that I have any particular problem with someone who does. What reading tarot has taught me is to listen to and trust my inner voice.

We all have that voice. Call it your conscience, or Jiminy Cricket, or Jesus, or Justin Timberlake; I don't care. We all have that voice, and I give heed to mine—the one that calls me "Child" —because I have learned that not doing so causes me problems by which I would just as soon not be troubled.

I said to DeLeon, "I need your help, if you're willing."

"Sure."

I asked him to wait for me in the dining room and went to get my cards out of their rose- and sandalwood box.

DeLeon knows I read cards, but he's never participated in a reading. Not everyone is comfortable around tarot cards, or around people who are reading them. I can't imagine why, except that these little pieces of colored cardboard seem to offend more restrictive and dogmatic religious leaders.

I don't like offending people's sensibilities if I can avoid it, so before I unwrapped the deck from its protective silk scarves I asked DeLeon, "Do you mind these? I'm being asked to read the cards but I can't read for myself very well. I don't remember what I've said afterward, so I need a witness."

"I haven't seen anyone read cards before, but I've heard folks say, 'can I get a witness' plenty of times." DeLeon smiled. "Whatever you need to do, Miz Ex, you go ahead on."

"What I need is for you to do your best to remember what I say, okay? When I read the cards I'm talking from someplace that doesn't consciously string words together, and I can't seem to restring them myself when I'm done. Afterward

I'm going to ask you about what I said."

"Got it. The 'record' button is lit up red." He touched his index finger to his forehead, between his eyebrows.

I unwrapped the cards and spread the scarves out on the table. I shuffled the deck until it warmed up from the heat of my hands. I split the oversized deck into three piles sitting on the top scarf, and felt like picking up the one on the right, so I did that and stacked it on top of the other two sections, reassembling the deck into a whole again.

"Am I allowed to ask questions?' I could hear tension in DeLeon's voice.

"You do whatever feels right to you. Ask me questions, comment on what you see on a card, tell me the thoughts that come to your mind as I'm speaking—anything at all.

"The Tarot is a tool for accessing our intuition. Because most deck designs are figurative, reading tarot is a little like interpreting dreams. A reader's job is to use her intuition to figure out what the pictures mean when they are arrayed in a layout with each other. But every source of information can be useful."

"Okay then."

I didn't bother to go into the many myths about the tarot, or that there are seventy-eight cards in a tarot deck, twenty-two of which are called the Major Arcana.

The Major Arcana represent the big cycles or phases life takes us through. The remaining fifty-six cards are the Minor Arcana, fourteen each in four different suits, and they are the precursors of today's playing cards. Put simply, the Minor Arcana tend to mean the day-to-day experiences of life.

In modern playing cards, Swords have been renamed Spades, Wands became Clubs, Cups became Hearts, and Pentacles became Diamonds.

There are many layouts for tarot readings, but this time I opted to put down a row of seven cards, from left to right. I use this layout when I want a snapshot of the situation. I was looking for any clues I could glean about what was happening or about to happen, without taking a lot of time.

In any reading, a higher or lower percentage of Major Arcana is worth noticing, because a high percentage can indicate that what's going on carries with it a sense that things are spiraling out of control.

In the layout I was looking at there was only one Major Arcanum: The High Priestess card. The predominance of Minor Arcana indicated the situation was one I could hope to grapple with without feeling overwhelmed.

I examined all the cards for a moment and

then began to talk. I have never been adept at "thinking" a reading.

The first card was the Princess of Cups, reversed, meaning upside down. Next was the Prince of Swords. The third card was the Five of Pentacles. In the center, reversed, was The High Priestess. The fifth spot was the Four of Cups. In the sixth place was the Seven of Cups. The last card was the Eight of Wands.

"DeLeon, this could be about Netta, or one of us, or me, okay? I'm going to ask for your help in figuring out what everything means. If I say something and you think it's wrong or off somehow, please say what comes to your mind and help me get back on track?"

"I'll do my best, Xana, given that I have no idea how this is supposed to work."

"Don't worry about it or overthink it. Just say what's in your mind."

"I don't seem to have any trouble with that," he laughed. "It's keepin' my opinions to myself that's the problem."

We smiled at each other. I could feel his nerves settling down, and that it was okay to start.

I pointed to the leftmost card: the Princess of Cups.

"She's reversed. When she's right-side up she's ready for a new adventure, something emotionally fulfilling. It could be anything that triggers that child-like feeling of enthusiasm and joy. But here she's upside-down, which often means someone who is immature and emotionally demanding."

I paused before I said what came to me next.

"DeLeon." I looked up at him. "Is there any chance Netta could be pregnant? And you can tell me it's none of my business."

DeLeon stared at me, disbelief on his face. He looked down and pointed at the Princess of Cups.

"You see that?"

"The thought that she was pregnant surfaced in my mind. When this card is right-side-up it can mean pregnancy. I don't know whether Netta is pregnant or not. When I'm reading cards I say what comes into my mind and I don't try to filter it. But you know more than I do about Netta."

He thought for a moment and shook his head.

"Maxine wouldn't tell me what they fussed about that got them both so mad. If it was about Netta bein' pregnant that would make sense. Maxine's been tryin' to talk sense to Netta about that boyfriend, but Netta never would listen."

"I don't know anything for a fact, okay? It was just a thought. There are other meanings I could be ignoring."

I didn't tell him that the other meanings tend to include drugs and alcohol.

I heard Thorne's footsteps upstairs. I knew he was packing up the printouts, tucking a thumb drive into the pocket of his dark gray jeans, checking that everything he'd found was e-mailed to the three of us so we would all have backup access to what he had learned.

"What else are you seein'?"

I pointed to the next card, the Prince of Swords.

"He's a whirlwind. He uses his intellect and his words to capture the minds of others. He creates momentum because he's obsessed with an idea. The downside of this card is that his ambition and drive can blind him to the difficulties, the damage, that his headlong pursuit of his goal can trigger."

"So this is a person?"

"It can be a person, or it can represent the way our psyche operates." I thought about it.

"My guess is that this is a person. I think maybe Netta met a young man and he talked to her for a while and he just swept her up with him. People like this are very compelling. They can be glamorous and captivating. At the same time, they can be heedless and cruel. They often use language as a weapon."

"Do you think this is the man she was seein'?"

"It could be. It could be someone more recent, or it can represent a pattern that Netta tends to fall into, of allowing herself to be captivated and carried away by someone who talks a great game."

DeLeon shook his head again. "Yes," he said. "Yes, yes."

"Let's look at the Five of Pentacles. In a couple of the tarot designs the image it shows is of two people, a man using a crutch and a woman with a shawl pulled over her head, walking in the snow outside a church. There's light shining through a stained glass window behind them. The card can refer to someone who insists on isolating herself, refusing the comfort and spiritual solace that are available to us all."

I thought about the card for a moment.

"This card can refer to a willful separation from family, friends, community. It may include a feeling of being unworthy, or of not deserving to be loved. When we were kids it was that whole 'nobody likes me, everybody hates me, I'm gonna go eat worms' thing."

"The week before she ran off Netta was sulkin' 'round the house, stayin' in her room, sleepin' long hours. I was havin' to push her to get up and off to school every day. Anything Maxine or I said, Netta acted like it was a big imposition to even listen."

I nodded in acknowledgement.

"This next card is the big one," I said. "It's the

High Priestess, and she's reversed. It's the only Major Arcana card, meaning 'big mystery,' and she's sitting here dead center. She's tough enough to figure out when she's straight up. Upside-down, wow."

I thought for a moment, allowing my intuition to bring words to the surface of consciousness.

"I think this card has links to the woman up in Marysville as well as into Netta's state of mind."

I paused. Whenever I do a reading for someone, there is meaning in the cards for me as well. Something was telling me to notice this card and figure out what it had to tell me.

"The High Priestess represents the link between our conscious and unconscious. She is our intuition, and when she shows up in a reading she is asking us to listen to our inner selves. But here she's reversed. Any reversed card indicates the potential for what the upright card means, but in this case I think she's here to warn us about a person who is refusing to listen anymore to her inner voice, her angels, if you will. She has shut down her intuition and is running her life based on willfulness and the assertion of false spiritual power."

If this card had something to say to me, I was at a loss to identify what that might be. I made an effort to open myself up to "hearing" what might be unwelcome news about myself.

I stopped and held my breath. I was frightened. I felt a shiver move up my back. My teeth chattered.

I disappeared from my dining room for a second, and saw a tall dark-haired woman with brilliant black eyes standing on a raised platform at one end of a large room. She was holding her hand out ahead of her, palm raised, as if blessing the rows of people seated on the floor below her. But her face was not kindly; her expression was hard and her eyes flashed with anger.

I felt DeLeon's hand squeeze mine.

"Miz Xana? Hey, there, Miz Ex?"

I forced my mind away from the hackle-raising woman in the vision and felt myself returning to the dining room. I took a deep breath and let it out slowly, releasing the fear that had overwhelmed me.

"Xana, where did you just go? You turned white as a snowflake. You white enough already, girl. I thought you were 'bout to pass out."

I laughed a jittery giggle, and he looked at me with alarm. Tears welled up in my eyes.

"DeLeon, we have to do something about her."

"Who you mean now?"

"The woman who has Netta. It's not enough to get Netta out of there. She's keeping them all prisoner. And they're all women."

"How do you know that?"

"Sometimes when I read cards I see things. I can't explain it."

He waved his hand over the cards.

"You want to finish this up, or what?"

I swallowed and clenched my teeth.

"Yes, I need to see what else there is. But I'm going to go faster. We have to get Netta out of there."

I heard rolling suitcase wheels on the carpet runner leading out of my bedroom. I was surprised by that. It meant Thorne thought it might take us more than today to retrieve Netta.

"You two an item now, yes?" DeLeon pointed to the ceiling. "About time, I'd say."

I smiled.

"There comes your color back. You blushin' like havin' a man at your age is embarrassin'."

"Don't tell my mother," I said. We both laughed.

DeLeon has met my mother. Everyone who meets my mother has the immediate urge not to tell her anything, but she possesses the irresistible power of seducing and/or compelling people into telling her whatever she is determined to know.

I have made it my business to get along with her. I don't know that she realizes what a daunting challenge that has proved to be.

I looked back down to the Four of Cups and

sighed.

"This card has a lot of meanings to sift through," I said, touching it.

"What's surfacing is the idea that we can become complacent about our blessings. We can be surrounded by love, with a roof over our heads and our health and plenty to eat, and still we're ungrateful. We don't accept that all the good things can and will slip away from us. We focus instead on what we want, but even if we get what we hoped for, a part of us realizes it won't make us any happier. This card is a reminder to express gratitude every day, I think."

"My Daddy used to tell me, 'Son, today is a new day. You should be thankin' the Lord for the time you've got, and that so far the Reaper's passed you by.'"

"Yes."

I smiled at DeLeon. Our shared look acknowledged the serendipity of our affection for each other.

I looked back down at the cards.

"The Four of Cups can mean more than what I'm focusing on, but I think Netta may be realizing that what she found in Marysville is nothing to be grateful for. She still may not realize how lucky she was before she went, but she does know that what she found there isn't what she wants."

I moved to the Seven of Cups.

"So many cards in the Cups suit. There's a lot of emotional stuff here. Which means this is about feeling more than thinking or doing. The Seven of Cups is considered to be about temptation, about being lured to explore what we might not normally get involved with, hoping to find new dreams that we think could or should come true."

I looked up at DeLeon. He nodded.

"There are risks here, though."

I tapped the card with a fingernail.

"We can live in dreamland instead of reality. We can fall in love with the dream and ignore the step-by-step actions necessary to bring the dream to reality. We can fail to see the downside of the dream, the snares and traps, the consequences that are cloaked from us when we get emotionally invested in something tempting."

"When we're young that's what we do. All horsepower and no brakes or steerin'."

"The last card is the Eight of Wands. Wands are fire, inspiration, creativity. This card is supposed to mean energy, rapid motion, air travel, focused and capable accomplishment. It's telling us to go fast, ready-aim-fire. But it's warning us to be careful and make sure everything is prepared. Look before we leap."

I thought about Thorne in the café, telling us to wait.

"Let's go."

DeLeon and I looked up, startled. Thorne had materialized in the doorway, the lintel an inch or two above his head. Binoculars hung around his neck. I gathered up the cards and pulled the scarves around them.

"I need to call Maxine and let her know what's happenin'." DeLeon pulled a cell phone out of a holster on his belt. "She can have Terrell cover tomorrow's clients."

"From the car," Thorne said. "We need to go now."

"I'll get the cooler," I said, meaning Thorne or DeLeon should get the cooler, since the cooler was a two-handed item to carry and I had one hand free and the other hand working a cane.

"In the car already."

There was a long drive ahead of us, and we'd be briefed on everything as we traveled, possibly including Thorne's plan. It would be a thoroughly amazing plan, and the plan would work.

But the image of the brilliant-eyed woman with the venomous expression haunted me.

I trusted Thorne, who is a mighty mighty man, but I was unnerved by the prospect of what awaited us up north.

Rightly so, as it turned out, and thus farewell, my tranquil mind.

≈4≈

"We're going past Marysville, along the Yuba River, east of where it converges with the Feather River," I said. "Three and a half hours, I'm estimating."

My roomy, leather-seated Chrysler 300C sedan rolled smoothly and quietly along Interstate 80 toward Sacramento.

For the last thirty minutes DeLeon had told Thorne and me about the card reading, and Thorne had walked us through the printouts and photographs.

We were passing the truck weighing station at Suisun, and the high sun streaming through the rear window warmed my shoulders.

We were driving my car in the hope that a blue American-made sedan would not stand out as glaringly as Thorne's black European luxury car among the pickups and tractors of rural Northern California.

With its awesome Hemi engine, the 300C would outrun just about any other vehicle we were likely to encounter that wasn't either a Lamborghini or manufactured to California Highway Patrol specifications.

"The Hemi is a safety feature," Thorne once told me, when I lead-footed it to get around a slow-moving truck.

I had come to realize during the first few miles of our trip that it was likely I would have to drive at some point. My car was an automatic. The BMW had a manual transmission, with a clutch that would test my less-than-full-strength left leg.

These were conclusions I had drawn. I hadn't bothered to verify any of my conclusions with Thorne. I would find out soon enough if what I had assumed was baseless.

Thorne metes out information as needed and no sooner. Plans change to meet changing circumstances in his world, so why talk about them before it's time to put them into motion?

DeLeon had offered to drive, since, of the two

men, he was the one with the driver's license. Thorne declined, pointing at the folders he'd prepared for us to peruse during the trip.

Once we cleared the East Bay traffic, he set the cruise control to five miles per hour over the speed limit. Other cars passed us going seventy-five or more.

Thorne doesn't care to make the acquaintance of law enforcement personnel. He lives off the grid entirely—no driver's license, no social security number, no bank account, no record of him anywhere after he left the Harvard MBA program. No contact with his disapproving and disappointed parents either.

He requires his personal security clients to pay him in cash. He does not receive a W-2 or 1099 at year-end, and no record is kept anywhere of his current phone number or address. I never have to look his phone number or address up, since he lives with me.

It's surprisingly difficult to survive without computerized ones and zeroes pinning you down in this Patriot-Acted, documented world, but he is Thorne and does exactly what he pleases. His BMW is registered in my name, paid for with cash Thorne stores in a safe in a storage locker somewhere, which cash is stacked alongside piles of the most adorably shiny gold coins and mini-ingots.

DeLeon and I rode in the back seat so we could compare folder contents. One of the printouts showed a photo of a beautiful young dark-haired woman with black eyes.

"That's who I saw," I said to DeLeon, pointing at the picture. "Only she was older and meaner-looking."

"She's good-lookin'."

"Did you read this one yet?' I pointed at a page.

"She was raised Catholic. Parochial schools. Sacred Heart and Marymount. Pushed for women priests when John Paul II started to roll back the Vatican reforms of John XXIII. Became an activist when Benedict was elected and all the child abuse cases were surfacing that he'd suppressed.

"When Benedict went after nuns, excommunicating the ones who disputed his edicts, she lapsed and started an alternative church in Marysville. She incorporated most of the Catholic mass, but she added elements from ancient goddess religions. Two years ago she declared herself *the* goddess."

"The blogs that ex-cult members are writin' say she's 'incredibly compelling when you first meet her,'" DeLeon said, pronouncing all the words precisely as he read them.

"'She demands that members renounce their prior lives and dedicate themselves to the true goddess.' If you challenge her on anythin' she puts you through her flavor of inquisition. I guess she's not seein' any irony in that, after her experience with the Pope?"

"How do they generate any income?" I asked Thorne.

"Farming. Roadside stand, farmers' market."

"Any idea how the town views them?" I asked.

"Harmless kooks."

"My impression, based on nothing but a momentary flip into a fugue state, is that she is anything but harmless," I said, looking at Thorne in the rear-view mirror. "And you said we needed to go right away, so you don't think she's harmless either. Why?"

"Missing man."

DeLeon and I thumbed through the stack of pages in the folder. He found the article first and held it for the two of us to read.

"Why so much attention to this guy goin' missin'?" DeLeon asked after he'd scanned it. "The article just say he left the cult. Couldn't he have joined another one and nobody can find him 'cause a that?"

"Look further down the page," I said. "The article says he left the cult because Renenet, originally Sharonna Rooney, got questioned by the police when the family found out where he'd gone and tried to locate him.

"She told the cops that the man left voluntari-ly. But the blogs about her cult say nobody leaves voluntarily, and that other people have gone missing. They say they had to sneak away or they would have disappeared, too."

Only after I spoke did I realize what I was saying, and the effect it would have.

"Are you sayin' she's killin' people who want to quit her group?' DeLeon's voice was sharp with anxiety.

"Whoa." Thorne held his right hand up in a "stop" gesture.

"We don't know that," I said.

"But Netta sent a message that she wanted out. Netta wants out."

"We'll get her. We'll be in time. She's smart. She found a way to send a message. Thorne will do what he does like nobody else, and you'll have your Netta back."

I tried to imbue my voice with as much con-viction as possible.

It didn't work.

"If that motherfuckin' bitch has hurt my child I'll kill her."

DeLeon's tone was matter-of-fact. He tapped the printed pages into a neat stack and slid them back into the manila folder. He pulled the driver's seatback pocket open and shoved the folder down into it. He was done thinking about the situation. It was too painful to consider the possibility that had surfaced and so DeLeon stopped considering anything at all.

He clasped his hands in his lap and stared sightlessly out the window at the cars rushing by in the other direction.

I looked over Thorne's shoulder at the speed-ometer. He had inched it up to seventy-five and reset the cruise control. We were still crawling compared to much of the traffic around us, but we were fifteen minutes closer to Marysville than we had been a moment ago.

ﭏ5ﭏ

My cell phone rang. The ringtone was "She Drives Me Crazy."

This is my mother's designated ringtone, my mother being the determinedly if not often happily married Mrs. Louisa Duncan Livingston Monaghan Bard, originally from Darien, Connecticut.

I hesitated about answering. I always hesitate before answering a call from "Mater," the epithet by which my four siblings and I all refer to her, except to her face.

From the front seat Thorne said, "Courage," the way the French pronounce it. It's a code word for us, meaning something along the lines of "suck it up and get on with it."

I answered the phone.

"Hi, Mother."

"Hello, Alexandra. I am driving up from Pebble,"—she meant Pebble Beach, where she has a house on the Monterey Peninsula Country Club golf course—"to San Francisco this Friday for a charity event DeDe is sponsoring. I have taken a table and I thought you could come and meet this nice attorney Charlotte knows who has just gotten a divorce. He is a partner in a big firm downtown. Charlotte has told him all about you and he is very interested in making your acquaintance. I will be staying with Ann, so you needn't get the guest room ready for me."

I was tempted to say, "I'm fine, thank you, and you?"

But I've tried that before, and it does not register with her. She is irreproachable, not because she doesn't deserve a little reproaching, but because she refuses to believe that anyone would attempt such an outrageous stunt with her.

"I'm afraid I'm busy this weekend. Perhaps another time."

I held out little hope that this mild refusal would carry the day, but I figured I'd start politely and work my way up to incivility.

"Alexandra, you know I do not ask much of you, and I know you enjoy DeDe and Charlotte. And Ann will be there too. You and she can talk about art. You know, you are not getting any more beautiful as time goes by, my dear. It wouldn't hurt you to meet someone new and be nice."

I ignored the insult. One must, with Mater. The fact is, I am not sure my mother doesn't know about Thorne, even though I have said nothing about him. I don't think Mater is above salting my neighborhood with paid observers, peppering them with inquiries and demanding reports two or three times a day about my movements and activities.

If Thorne didn't regularly scan the premises for bugs and cameras I'd wonder if Mater hadn't rigged my house for twenty-four hour sur-veillance. She likes to "stay in touch," as she phrases it.

"Mother, recently divorced men are not known for being great long-term prospects. And every attorney I have ever dated enjoys arguing as his favorite pastime. For attorneys, losing an argument means losing income, which is anathe-ma. It has always been my preference to get along amicably with my date *du jour*, sans disputation.

"Besides, you know that DeDe and Charlotte and Ann will all be focusing on the rich donors at the event so they can nail down the big bucks they're trying to raise. Your friends are charming, and they will say an expensively perfumed hello to me and promptly shift their attention to the CEO of McKesson. So I appreciate the effort, and please thank Charlotte for her thoughtfulness, but I won't be able to attend on Friday. I am out of town right now."

Which was not a lie. I am scrupulous about lying to her, since one of Mater's gifts is an unerring bullshit detector. I think there is a recessive gene for it.

DeLeon curled his hands into fists and bent his elbows into a flexed-bicep pose. He was encouraging me to stay strong. I rolled my eyes and waited for the next onslaught.

"Oh. Where are you?" Mater said.

"Heading north. I'm on the way to Tahoe."

Again, not a lie. We hadn't turned off of Highway 80 yet.

"What on earth for? You are not going gambling, are you?"

I thought of our expedition and decided that with Thorne in charge, nothing was a gamble.

"No, Mother."

"Then what on earth are you going to Tahoe for?"

Mater hangs on like a mongoose severing the spine of a cobra when she is on a quest for information.

"We're going to visit some family friends. They're staying up north."

"Who are 'we'?"

Oops.

"DeLeon, Mother."

I spoke in the resigned tone of the found-out. Mater does not approve of DeLeon. He is wealthy enough to pass muster, but he is not a member of the Olympic and Bohemian Clubs.

"That soundless hoodlum of yours is with you, isn't he?"

So she did know about Thorne.

"Mother, who I'm friends with is not your decision to make. And if I were going somewhere with Thorne Ardall, which is his name and I wish you would use it, why would I tell you, when that's the way you characterize him? You have to stop imagining you can make my choices for me."

"I do not have to stop doing any such thing. You are my daughter and I am entitled to be concerned for your welfare. And it is not as if your past choices have been so marvelous."

"Mother—" I began to make gargly scratchy noises in my throat.

"I'm losing. . . signal. . . can't hear. . ."

I hit Stop on the cell phone to end the call. I turned the phone's power off. I would worry about voice mail messages later.

I reached through the gap between the front seats and slid the phone into the convenient slot next to the gearshift.

Everything in me wanted to open the window and hurl the phone out onto the freeway so I could watch it shatter into a squillion little shards—maybe even be run over by all eighteen wheels of a semi—never to receive a call from Mater ever again. But my Mother wasn't the phone's fault and the phone didn't deserve to die for being the conduit for her verbal antics. Hence the transfer of the blameless device into Thorne's arena, from which location I would arrange to keep myself clear until I no longer felt like pulverizing the little fella.

"You forgot to give her my love," DeLeon said.

"Ditto," said Thorne.

They kept extremely straight faces as they spoke.

Then we all burst out laughing, and we laughed like crazy people.

Which, given the venture we had embarked on, was hardly debatable.

≈⌗≈

Route 70 transitions from freeway to town streets when it passes through Marysville, and we crawled along from traffic signal to traffic signal until we were halfway past Ellis Lake. At mid-town we turned off to the northeast on Highway 20. By now it was getting on in the afternoon.

We stopped for fuel and rest rooms. I gave Thorne my ATM card and he did the honors at the gas pump. We would want to get the hell out of Dodge once we gathered up Netta, and the car would need a full tank to get home on without stopping. The Hemi, while zippy as all get-out, does not have a hybrid's stamina, mileage-wise.

We pulled out of the station and drove another four or five minutes along Highway 20, past orchards and cultivated fields. California poppies lit the highway verge passing by on either side of us like flickers of cold flame.

"Destination," the GPS voice said. On the right side of the rural highway was an open-fronted farm stand with a green wooden awning, RENENET FARM ORGANIC PRODUCE lettered across it. Two women wearing yellow aprons over their clothes stood behind the countertop, baskets of vegetables and cardboard egg cartons sitting on a slant in front of them.

Starting on the near side of the stand a fifty-yard dirt and gravel driveway ran back to the farm buildings, with grass and weeds growing between the tire tracks.

At the end of the rutted driveway stood a huge four-story gabled white farmhouse surrounded by tall shade trees. Another thirty yards behind the farmhouse loomed a red barn. Alongside the barn was a chicken wire fence enclosing a large coop and a couple of dozen colorful chickens.

In a fenced pasture next to the barn were two black draft horses with white forelegs and face blazes. Shires, they looked like to me.

I grew up taking riding lessons; Mater felt it behooved us, as it were, to know a fetlock from a pastern and to "have a good seat."

Riding allowed me time to myself, time in nature, time with the dainty, dappled gray Apolina, who made no disparaging comments about the lack of crispness in my riding jacket or my unpolished riding boots.

Every so often a rustling leaf or chirping bird would cause Apolina to jump around like she was on crack, but that was expected Arab temperament; it just made the ride more diverting.

I brought my attention back to the Marysville farm. A hundred feet or so from the horse corral loomed a long, ten-foot-high mound covered by an equally long green tarp, the tarp held down by car tires along the edges. A similar mound, uncovered and carved into from one end, sat a few yards away from it. Seasoned horse manure and compost for the farm, if I guessed right.

The traffic on the road was intermittent and consisted almost entirely of pickup trucks. Big, small, battered, brand-new, none of them looking at all like the sleek dark blue sedan we rode in. The non-pickup trucks tended to be small Japanese-logo sedans. So much for our efforts not to have our vehicle stand out.

Thorne slowed the car as we passed the produce stand and then drove on for another hundred yards, pulling off into a grove of trees on the same side of the road as the farm. He lowered all the windows and turned off the ignition.

There was no sound except for the birds in the trees around us and the occasional vehicle passing by on the road. The hot afternoon air poured into the car.

I smelled dirt and manure and the pervasive tang of garlic growing in the field behind the produce stand.

Vehicles were pulling into and out of the parking area in front of the produce stand. People walked into the awning's shade and pointed at what they wanted to buy. Others picked up their bagged purchases and left.

Thorne picked up the binoculars from the passenger side floor and looked at the farm. From our vantage point we could see the cultivated fields behind the barn as well as those between the house and the highway. Behind the cultivated vegetable fields was an orchard.

I could see a couple of dozen people working one cultivated field. Thorne was scanning them quickly and carefully.

DeLeon was holding his breath. We both knew better than to speak.

"There," said Thorne, handing the binoculars to DeLeon and pointing. "Ten o'clock, orange tank top, black do-rag."

I sighed with relief.

DeLeon moved the binoculars back and forth

and then held them still. He made a noise not un-like a growl and kept the binoculars up to his eyes.

"Sweet Jesus, there she is, she's all right." His voice shook.

I had spotted the far-off person he was look-ing at, her head bent so that she faced the dirt. Her dark brown arms were bare in the neon or-ange tank top, and she was stepping slowly and rhythmically, dropping and dragging a hoe as she moved along a row of what looked like strawber-ry plants.

"What now?" I asked Thorne, as he climbed out of the car. He leaned in the door to look at me.

"You're driving."

I grabbed my cane and clambered out of the car, walked around the front to the driver's door, and awaited further instructions.

Thorne walked to the back of the car, took out a multi-purpose pocket gadget, and hunkered down. I heard him unscrewing the license plate. He walked forward and slid the plate under the driver's seat.

Thorne reached over into the passenger floor area, picked up his running shoes, and sat side-ways in the driver's seat with his feet out the door. He swapped his buff-colored work boots for the running shoes.

I saw it now. Thorne would fetch Netta from

the field and DeLeon would want to sit with her on the way home, so Thorne needed me to be wheelwoman. He had removed the license plate so any pursuers could not track us down by the plate number.

I have learned to rely on my experience with Thorne, and not to ask for an explanation when time is of the essence. The afternoon was growing late, and there was no predicting how long the workers would stay out tilling the field.

DeLeon opened his door and put his boot on the ground to go along.

Thorne stood up in front of him, holding out his hands and blocking DeLeon's way.

"No," he said.

"What?" DeLeon demanded.

"DeLeon, look around at everyone you see," I said. "Thorne has to do this part for you. And Netta knows him. She'll go with him. And meanwhile, how fast can you run?" I pointed at his cowboy boots.

DeLeon, in his black suit and jazzy tie, with his brown skin and kinked hair in a ponytail, would attract an exorbitant amount of attention before he could reach Netta.

"I could run *real* fast if I thought this one was chasin' me," DeLeon said, flicking his thumb sideways at Thorne.

I laughed, and the corner of Thorne's mouth

twitched upward. The tension went out of the confrontation.

Thorne, a Caucasian wearing jeans and Nikes, would not exactly fit in, but he would blend in a lot better than DeLeon. Besides which, Thorne could be lumbered with swim fins on his feet and still outrun everybody except maybe Usain Bolt.

"I want to help," DeLeon said.

"You will," Thorne answered, and turned to me where I was standing beside the driver's door.

"When I have Netta, drive fast to the barn. Aim back out again."

"When you grab Netta, get to the barn and turn around, doors open, in gear and ready to hit it hard."

He nodded and held his hand against my cheek. I leaned my chin into the tough heel of his hand and gazed up at him. Thorne is not big on public displays of affection. For him, in front of observers, cheek cradling and an intense gaze are the limit.

We trust each other entirely. The look was full of love and awareness and appreciation, plus a rather splendid mind-meld that I have come to realize is both reliable for us and rather rare among other humans.

Thorne dropped his hand and lifted his gaze, scanned around him, and moved swiftly out of the trees to the two-lane highway. He jogged along the dirt shoulder toward the produce stand.

DeLeon sat down into the back seat, pulled his legs into the car, and shut his door. He picked up the binoculars and stared at his daughter, as if his unrelenting gaze could keep her safe.

I sat in the driver's seat and touched the button that would adjust it to my settings from Thorne's. I fastened the seat belt, started the car, checked the mirrors, and watched Thorne with his long strides running effortlessly, rapidly, the way he could for twenty miles.

I left the car windows down, listening for I don't know what. I thought I'd know what I was listening for if I heard it. I shut off the air conditioning rather than try to cool the entire town of Marysville.

I put the car in gear and turned it around so we faced the highway. I watched my mighty mighty man running toward the people buying vegetables.

Thorne disappeared behind the produce stand for a moment as he turned down the driveway. He reappeared with a hoe angled over his shoulder and continued running down the driveway toward the tall white farmhouse.

Thorne passed behind the barn and took off in high gear across the field rows toward Netta, charging with the intensity and what seemed like the speed of a cheetah.

The women he passed stood up and stopped working, watching him leap over the raised rows of strawberries. He held the hoe cradled in his elbow like a knight's lance.

Netta stopped working, stood up straight, and turned to look at him. I heard her high-pitched shout.

She dropped her hoe, held up her arms, and stumbled across the field rows toward her liberator.

A loud bell rang out from somewhere on the farm.

I pressed the accelerator and the Hemi kicked in, whipping our heads against the headrests as we surged out onto the highway, tires screeching on the pavement.

We just about achieved lift-off, wind whipping through the car windows, barreling toward the barn that stood between DeLeon and his daughter.

≋7≋

Thorne snatched Netta up as if she were a toddler and hoisted her onto his hip. She wrapped her legs around his waist and her arms around his neck. He held her waist with one arm and the hoe with the other, veering and hot-footing it back toward the barn.

I turned into the driveway and lost sight of them behind the barn, but I heard more shouts from the direction of the field. I floored it down the driveway. The sound of the bell, clanging like a burglar alarm, grew louder as I neared the barn.

Passing the farmhouse as Thorne and Netta reappeared around the corner of the barn, I put the car into a power skid that slued the car around. When we came to a stop we were aimed back out toward the street, ten yards or so away from the two runners.

"Doors!" I yelled at DeLeon, but he was already pushing open the rear passenger door, standing up and holding out his arms to grab Netta.

A thirty-ish, freckle-faced, auburn-haired man was leading a pack of women chasing the fugitives. He was carrying a pitchfork, holding the sharp tines out in front of him. The running women carried hoes and hand-rakes.

I had a momentary zombie-movie flashback, and then remembered the image of the Knight of Swords on his galloping white horse. The wicked wordsmith, I thought, must be the one with the pitchfork.

Thorne released Netta and DeLeon threw her into the back seat. As she scrambled across to the other side of the car, Thorne turned and hurled his hoe handle-first like a javelin at the Knight of Swords, who swung his pitchfork to bat it away.

He missed, and the hoe hit him squarely in the chest. He staggered, diverting the attention of the charging crowd of women, who halted to help him stay upright.

DeLeon jumped in behind Netta, blocking her from the pursuers, and Thorne threw himself into the front passenger seat.

I did not need to be urged by Eliza Doolittle to "move my bloomin' arse."

I jammed the accelerator to the floorboard and the car doors slammed shut as we took off. The rear wheels spun a rooster tail of dirt and pebbles at the group chasing us. They turned their backs to shield themselves as we fish-tailed away, gathering speed down the driveway toward the produce stand and Route 20.

I thought it possible that the two women in yellow aprons would try to block our exit, and lucky for them that they and their customers just gaped as we flew by. I was pumped so full of adrenaline that I'd have flattened them all and been glad to do it.

The car squealed left onto the highway and I aimed us back toward town. Once on the straightaway I closed all the windows and Thorne turned on the air conditioning.

DeLeon was holding Netta tightly, their heads close together. He was saying indecipherable things to her, sounding mostly like, "Shhh, shhh, sweetheart, shhh, shhh." She was sobbing, clinging to him, saying "Daddy," again and again.

"Silver truck," Thorne said. He had turned and was keeping a lookout through the rear window. In the side mirror I saw a big four-by-four pickup truck pulling out of the farm driveway, coming after us.

Since we met, Thorne has made something of a project out of me, which I must say is a refreshing change. My romantic history reflects a penchant for fixing up a series of wounded birds who, once fixed up, fly away from the nest with nary a chirp of gratitude.

They promptly crash, of course.

Hey, at least I don't take them back.

Thorne was literally instead of figuratively wounded when we met, but has since evinced zero need for my intervention. Instead, he is sprucing me up. I have to say I am enjoying his form of TLC.

I know I was fine before, but I am definitely finer now.

He has paid for me to take the Bondurant School driver training for security professionals. He has also coached me in Aikido and Krav-Maga martial arts, and is needling me in his taciturn way to begin learning about and practicing using firearms.

I loved learning high-performance driving and self-defense, with the resulting boosts to my confidence. So far I have failed to agree about the shooting. They're noisy and smelly, is my take on guns.

The day may come, though, when noisy and smelly are no longer worth ignoring, and no person is more contemplatively patient in the face of stalwart ignoring than Thorne.

Route 20 ran straight back toward town. The truck couldn't catch us if I kept my foot down, but it's one thing to outmaneuver pursuit on a closed racetrack; it's another thing entirely to attempt it on a two-lane road outside a small town that is likely to post speed traps and cops at each end to catch out-of-towners like me.

Folks who can be made to pay big bucks for the mistake of going five miles per hour over the posted limit are major contributors to city and county tax revenues in California, or maybe in every state.

Thorne turned on the car's GPS so that it showed the local map. We were approaching the town, with rows of residential housing on the right.

"Turn right," he said.

I turned right. The tires shrieked but the car was heavy with passengers and mostly held the pavement; I had to overcorrect the steering a little. If the silver truck with its higher center of gravity tried the same turn at the same speed, it would roll.

"Weave," Thorne said, so I wove.

Nadene Drive, Johnson Avenue, Del Pero Street. I put multiple turns and view-obscuring houses between us and the pursuing truck.

"Won't he figure out that we're on our way

back to the City? Why won't he just go sit where Highway 70 becomes a freeway again and wait for us?"

"He will."

"Then why are we doing this?"

I turned another corner.

"Park and wait until dark," he said.

"Now?"

He nodded. I saw a house with a hedge along one side of the driveway and a fence on the other. I slowed to look, and there were no cars parked at home. I backed in, so we could drive straight out when the time came. Our car was out of sight now unless someone stopped directly in front of the driveway and looked. I hoped the residents were away and the neighbors were not nosy.

When the engine stopped, Netta's grubby hand reached up from the back seat. I took it, noticing dirt and broken fingernails and blisters, and I kissed it. She patted Thorne's shoulder and pulled her hand back again, and nestled against her father.

DeLeon wrapped his arm around her, pulling her tightly to him. She reeked of hard physical labor minus any recent bathing. DeLeon clearly did not care about that. None of us cared about that.

"Trunk," Thorne said.

I pressed the trunk latch button and handed

him the license plate. He took it, climbed out, went to the back of the car, and reattached the plate to the bumper. Then he lifted the trunk lid, pulled out the canvas car cover, and shook it open.

I rolled down my window. "How are you going to get back in if you put that on the car?"

"I'm not."

"May I have the paper towels and the food, please?" I said, and from the trunk where I keep the towels he brought the roll and the cooler.

Thorne hurled the cover like a fisherman hurls a net and pulled the canvas down over the car's hood and doors. He would keep watch while we waited for dusk.

We sat quietly, in the tan gloom inside the canvas shroud. I opened a bottle of water that was sitting in the cup holder and soaked a wad of paper towels.

"For you, sweetie."

I handed them back to Netta and smiled at her. She scrubbed her face and hands with the towels and put the wadded-up gray remains into the empty plastic bag I keep in the car for trash.

I offered Netta a sandwich from the cooler on the front passenger seat, and some more water. She ate two sandwiches, moaning sometimes between bites, and drank a bottle of water. When she had finished eating she said, "Thank you,

Auntie Ex."

While she ate, DeLeon called Maxine to let her know the good news. He held the phone away from his ear when she made that noise women sometimes make, the high-pitched bat shriek that signals the first moments of a reunion with old friends, a baby shower prize, or the presence of a boy band.

Thorne, the master planner, had packed bath towels. Netta folded one into a pillow. DeLeon patted his legs and she put the towel on them, bending to rest her head on her father's lap, curling up into fetal position on the wide back seat. DeLeon carefully unknotted her do-rag and stroked her hair lightly. In a minute or two she was asleep.

When darkness fell I drove us back to San Francisco. We did not encounter the silver truck or any of the zombie-chasing populace along the way.

So I thought it was all over.

≈8≈

Netta sat across from me in DeLeon's dining room, her eyes cast down at the floor. DeLeon sat on the edge of the chair next to me, gazing at his daughter, his hand stretched out across the tabletop toward her.

Thorne was in the kitchen with Maxine. I could hear Maxine talking to him as dishes clinked into the dishwasher, her voice occasionally throbbing with emotion. I couldn't hear Thorne, but then Thorne mostly listens.

Scanning for anything troubling, Thorne had left the house from time to time during the evening to walk the perimeter of the block where DeLeon's family lives in the Oakland hills.

Because Netta had taken a house key and ID with her when she ran away, Thorne called an associate who had, with a team of helpers, already changed the locks and installed a state-of-the-art security system.

The clock in the living room chimed eleven times. Outside the traffic sounds on Piedmont Avenue died down and the night was quiet.

Netta showered until the hot water ran out as soon as she walked into the house, or as soon as Maxine had spun down to a halt from her screaming, cast-iron embrace of her grungy prodigal daughter.

Netta stood passively at first, enduring the embrace but not participating, and then slowly her arms came up and around her mother. They both wept, Netta silently and shakily, Maxine fiercely and scoldingly.

As soon as she had heard that Netta was on her way home, Maxine had cooked, the way she always did when she was happy, stressed out, bored, or anything at all.

I go to the beach and stare at the ocean under similar conditions. Staring at the Pacific is not as tasty, but it is also less fattening than Maxine's macaroni and cheese with a side of greens, followed by peach cobbler with ice cream. Tomorrow I would have to walk on the beach instead of just staring at it.

Netta had not spoken during the meal. Now, clean and fed and wearing fresh jeans and a sweatshirt, her still-damp hair twisted up into a knot on top of her head, she looked up at me from across the table.

"Why are you the one asking me questions?" she said.

"Netta," said DeLeon.

He had changed out of his suit and tie into jeans and a long-sleeved knit shirt. I touched his shoulder gently and he was quiet.

"Because your Mom and Dad thought you might be more at ease talking to me," I said.

"Are you with him for real?' She pointed toward the kitchen.

She had met Thorne once at a Labor Day barbecue in her backyard, but DeLeon had introduced him to her. It was an eclectic assortment of folks at the party, and Thorne and I hadn't been the only white guests attending. I don't think Netta had put the two of us together until now.

"Yes," I said.

"He's like the Hulk or something."

"Yes."

"He just snatched me up. He scared the shit out of me."

"Netta."

She looked at her father and shrugged.

"Well, he did."

"Thorne can be a very scary dude," I said.

"When I saw him I figured Daddy sent him."

"Yes. Your dad came looking for Thorne as soon as he got the note from your friend. You were smart to figure out a way to send it."

"I had to sneak around to get me some paper and a pen. One day when the regular lady was sick they told me to carry some vegetables up to the stand. I waited until Billie and Marge weren't watching and I took coins from the cash box. I came around the back of the stand and gave the envelope and the money for the stamp to a lady who was going back to her car. I wasn't sure she'd mail it. But Billie saw me hand the letter to the lady and she told Finn. After that—" she stopped and swallowed.

"After that I wasn't allowed to take vegetables up to the stand anymore," she finished. She was looking down at the floor again.

"Who is Finn? We saw mostly women at the farm," I said.

"He's the one who talked me into going up there with him. The one your boyfriend hit with the hoe. I think he's the one brings all the women in for Renenet."

"How did you two meet?"

"At the bus station. I was sitting waiting for the bus to L.A. First this pimp came up and hit on me and I kept telling him to go away, but he wouldn't leave me alone. Finn came over and stepped between us and started yelling, the way white boys can do at a brother without anybody thinking you should arrest the white boy and not the brother. Some other folks joined in and the pimp gave up and took off."

"And you and Finn struck up a conversation?"

"Yeah. He was white, you know? Wearing jeans and a shirt and a leather jacket. So I didn't think he was just another pimp."

"But he was," DeLeon said.

"Yes," Netta said, quietly, hanging her head.

DeLeon and I waited while Netta shed more tears. I had brought a box of tissues from the bathroom and I pushed them closer to her. She yanked two out and held them to her eyes and nose.

"DeLeon, could you give me a moment with Netta, please? I think she and I need a little time for some girl talk."

I don't think any father wants to hear what I thought Netta might say next.

DeLeon's face, thick with suffering, both reproached and thanked me for wanting to shield him from knowing the specifics of what had happened to Netta. He stood, bent to kiss his daughter on top of her head, and went to the kitchen. He shut the door behind him.

He trusted me to tell him what he needed to know. I was not looking forward to finding out what happened, but it needed to be done, and the weight of DeLeon's trust was worth bearing if it would help him and Netta and Maxine.

I moved around the table to sit next to Netta. I think it may be easier for some people to say difficult things without making eye contact.

I put my arm lightly around her shoulders and put my other hand on her arm that was closest to me. I spoke softly, close to her ear.

"Tell me what you can, sweetie."

She started shaking. I held her tighter.

"Only what you can manage," I whispered. "You're strong, you know. You got yourself home safe again. You're all right now. So you just take your time and tell me what you can."

Slowly, for the next hour, stopping and starting, both of us weeping intermittently, she told me.

ג ג ג

Netta asked me to keep her story in confidence, but I couldn't promise her that.

She was a sixteen-year-old girl who had acted as stupidly as it was possible to do, and had nonetheless managed to extricate herself, with help, from the appalling predicament that resulted.

I thought she needed a rehearsal with a non-

parent in order to work her way up to the necessary conversation with her mother and father, but
I knew the parental conversation was essential,
given what had happened to her.

I was overstepping and meddling by hearing
the story first, and I knew it, and I was not feeling
good about it, but the story was out and could be
dealt with now.

After Netta talked herself into silence with
me, I apologized to DeLeon and Maxine for my
interference, explained what Netta had asked for,
offered what I thought was the right thing to do
based on what she'd told me, and left it to them to
decide.

I was surprised when Maxine, holding DeLeon's hand, said, "You and Thorne brought her
back to us. I don't know that I want to find out
anything more than that my baby is back home
safe."

She put her arm around her daughter. DeLeon
turned to Netta and caressed her hair, then pulled
her into a family embrace.

"Baby, if you need help we'll get you help,"
he said. "We love you and there are no words for
how happy we are to have you back home again.
You can say anything to us and we will listen."

He lifted his eyes to me. "I think we should
just let Netta rest first."

Maxine nodded.

"Thank you for what you have done for my family," DeLeon said to Thorne, holding out his hand for Thorne to shake the traditional way.

DeLeon and Maxine were still in shock, I think. If I were Netta's parents I don't know that I would have allowed someone else to be the first to learn what had really happened to my daughter. I think I would feel compelled to call out the forces of retribution and mayhem without further delay. But it was the wee hours by now, and all of us except Thorne were exhausted beyond our ability to think very clearly.

As we stood there, Netta's brother Terrell, having driven the Escalade for a visiting celebrity all day and into the night, burst through the front door. Terrell and Netta were still hugging each other when Thorne and I departed. Maxine was heading to the kitchen to cook up something delicious for her family.

Thorne drove us across the Bay Bridge back to the City. The dashboard clock read one-seventeen as we came out of the Yerba Buena Island tunnel.

Lights from the City's downtown high-rises glinted through the darkness and fog on our right. We were both silent as the tires thumped rhythmically over the roadway sections.

It had been a very long day. I stared at the City lights, thinking about the awful story Netta had recounted. Thorne, noticing everything the way he does, reached over, took my hand, and held it all the way across town.

Rather than stop and start along the tedious, curveless commercial stretch of Geary Boulevard, he took the sinuous JFK Drive through the fifty-block dark green length of Golden Gate Park.

He knows I like to see the shaggy buffalo in their pasture just before 41st Avenue, and also the Dutch windmill right where the park meets the ocean.

It was too dark to see any buffalo, but the tulips at the windmill were blooming and their orderly ranks of yellow and orange and red were a bright gleam in the darkness.

As we swung right from the Great Highway onto 48th Avenue I finally spoke.

"It's not over, is it?"

"No."

"Will they come for her?"

"How bad was it?' He meant Netta's mistreatment in Marysville.

"Beyond bad."

"If they figure on law enforcement."

What he meant was, the Marysville cult might very well take preventive action against DeLeon's family to avoid prosecution.

Thorne pushed the garage door button and waited as the door retreated upward.

"It's not my decision what to do next," I said,

as he drove the car carefully into the garage, a couple of inches to spare on either side of the mirrors.

What I really meant was, "I'm not willing to let go of this matter."

He shut off the engine and pushed the button again to lower the garage door. We sat in the car, listening to the ticking of the cooling engine and waiting for the automatic light to go out. We both like to sit in the car in the dark, holding hands and talking. Or not talking.

"How much time do you think we have?" I said.

He turned and looked at me. The light was still on and I could see his face. I perceived his look to mean, "Not much."

What Thorne actually said was, "Sleep."

≈*9*≈

Sunlight haloed the bedroom's black curtains when I awoke. Thorne was gone, but he was generally gone long before I awoke on any given day. He was probably running the dogs up around Land's End or the old Presidio, if I needed to find him.

Our living arrangement may seem odd to others, but it works for us. He has his own "apartment" on the ground floor, on the western side of the house that backs up against the fenced Japanese garden. His space consists of a compact bedroom, bathroom, and kitchen/dining/living area.

Thorne uses a separate entrance from the one that leads to the two upper floors that are "mine."

Our arrangement permits us to back away into our neutral corners as needed, reconnecting when we feel like being in each other's company.

I own the house free and clear, and I pay the property taxes and insurance. Thorne buys all the groceries, since he is the only one who cooks. He restocks his and my refrigerators and makes sure there is an adequate supply of pet food and dark chocolate at all times. Also bacon.

We divvy up other expenses reasonably evenly, and neither one of us keeps track, nor does either one of us really have to keep track for financial reasons. I was the beneficiary of a very large legal settlement some years ago, and Thorne has the doubloon-filled safe that he replenishes whenever he is body-guarding someone richer than a Saudi princeling.

The cats aren't asking to go to Bennington next year and I'm not mainlining heroin, so the legal settlement has lasted me longer than it might someone who has college-bound kids, a mortgage, and a heroin habit.

One day I may have to go out and seek some sort of gainful employment again, but that day has not yet arrived and I have learned to like it like that. Since losing my day job I have acquired the skill of enjoying my own company, and now Thorne's, and of course there is the solid representation of amusing canine and feline denizens around the homestead.

I lay in bed studying the ceiling and pondering what I might do with the new day. It was a Thursday, and I had no particular plan other than to check in with DeLeon to see how Netta was doing. I intended to ask whether she had started talking about what she had gone through.

Thorne would want to check in with them about the possibility of cult retaliation, but for now the Oakland hills house was equipped with so much security equipment that Renenet would have to use a laser-guided smart bomb to get at Netta.

The phone on the nightstand rang. I thought it might be DeLeon or even Thorne, who, when he wants to communicate, sometimes rings up from downstairs rather than make the two-floor hike.

In any case I picked the handset up all unawares.

It was Mater.

"Hello, Mother, what a nice surprise."

I consciously stifled the threat of sourness in my tone.

"How are you?"

"I am well, Alexandra dear. I was wondering if you were by any chance back in town."

It was not a question. She really had to have spies planted like juniper shrubs all over my neighborhood.

"As a matter of fact I am." I dreaded the rest of the conversation.

"Dear, you know I so rarely ask anything of you," she said, which was a riot but I managed not to laugh.

"The thing is, I really am in quite a pickle or I wouldn't trouble you."

"What sort of pickle are we talking about?"

"There has been a cancellation at my table for tomorrow night's charity dinner-dance. The one that DeDe is sponsoring? Evvie Kiskaddon has the flu, so she and Maurice will not be able to attend."

Mater pronounced his name "Morris." There was silence as I thought about what to say.

"Mother, when you were at Sacred Heart did you know someone named Sharonna Rooney? Tall, dark hair, striking, with dark beautiful eyes?"

"Why on earth are you asking me that?"

She sounded affronted.

"Please, humor me. Do you remember her?"

"I would have to think about it. Or unearth the yearbook from somewhere. Is it that important?"

"It is if you want me to fill in tomorrow night."

Manipulation and shameless emotional blackmail are my mother's favorite languages, and I, having learned from a master, speak them fluently when the need arises.

"Oh, all right. I'll see if I can scare up my yearbook from wherever I might have put it. Can it wait until tomorrow night?"

"Yes. And I'll bring a plus one, so your two empty places at the table are now occupied."

"Who will you be bringing, dear?"

There was an edge to her question, which I ignored.

"For the seating chart when you arrive," she added.

"I'm not quite sure yet, but I will find some-one."

"It's black tie, dear."

She was implying that if I brought my mute gargantuan friend he could not possibly manage to be properly attired.

"I'll be sure to wear a tux."

"Oh, Alexandra. Sometimes I just don't know what to say to you."

"'Thank you' is always the correct choice, I think, when someone is doing you a favor."

I was being impolite, I know. I tend to lose my manners when Mater triggers all the launch codes.

She paused. For the last year or so Mater has been grappling with my more self-assured and, well, impolite responses to her remarks.

Which is splendid, in my opinion. I want to have good relationships with my family, and I don't think good relationships flourish by allowing family members to verbally mistreat me at will.

"Yes, of course, thank you, Alexandra. The gala is at eight o'clock at the Saint Francis. I shall look forward to seeing you there."

We said goodbye and I rolled over and out of bed. I had a plan for the day now, and that plan was to determine whether tuxedos were manufactured in "mute gargantuan" size.

I also needed to find a dress to wear, and some very high heels. The mended ankle was bolted together for all eternity, but I was willing to break the other ankle if it meant I could play dress-up and go to the ball with my oversized prince.

On our fancy date I planned to gather information about the "goddess incarnate of prosperity and abundance" whose "people are her children." Her captive and abused children.

Here is how the conversation went, as Thorne and I sat eating our "Sin Man Fresh Tossed" at the East-West café:

"Do you have or can you arrange for access to a tuxedo by tomorrow night?"

"With or without patent leather evening shoes?"

"Whichever."

"Yes."

I was Gomer Pyled into saying "Surprise, sur-prise," and then I refocused on the correct balance between real maple syrup, butter and cinnamon on what folks who don't value creativity would call French Toast.

I pondered for a moment the concept of bat-tleship-sized patent leather men's evening pumps. Then I thought about having some dark chocolate with my Fresh Tossed, but I opted for bacon instead.

≈10≈

"Alexandra, darling, you look as lovely as always."

"Thank you DeDe. Let me introduce you to Thorne Ardall. Thorne Ardall, our hostess, DeDe Ironhorse."

DeDe looked up at Thorne's impassive face from her five-foot-four inches to his six-foot-eight. She held out her hand and it disappeared into his. I think she was going to curtsey, but she caught herself and blushed instead.

"Enchanted," he said, meeting her gaze quietly, holding it until she finally pulled her hand away and turned to me.

"Louisa is here already, dear," she said, pointing me to a table near the dais at the far end of the ballroom.

"Thank you, DeDe. Your gown is unbelievably elegant. More so because you're wearing it." Her dress was black lace over a spaghetti-strap underdress, with beading that sparkled in the flatteringly dim lighting.

"Thank you, my love. You look even more gorgeous than usual. Now let me greet my other guests and we'll chat later."

Thorne and I strolled into the ballroom, my left arm gripping his right one because he was steadying me on my unpredictable left ankle.

I had abandoned the unglamorous cane in the car. I thought of FDR with an iron grip on his son's elbow as he pretended to walk for the cameras.

A dance band was playing, but people turned to look at us and conversations lulled. Wearing platform heels and with my blonde hair in an updo, I was over six feet tall. I had dabbed on a little eye makeup, and I was wearing a strapless gown of smoky blue silk georgette over matching satin crèpe.

Thorne, with his hair gelled off his forehead into a fixed style rather than his usual mop, was a dinner-jacketed behemoth, and a very elegantly turned-out behemoth if I may say so. For footwear he had chosen mirror-shined lace-ups in lieu of patent leather pumps.

I have to admit I wondered whether it was actually possible to own a pair of size 16EEE patent leather evening shoes, but I don't think I would actually like to see such a wonder.

Apparently the rich folks he protects for a living go to parties like this one with some frequency, and his custom-made tuxedo was simply the protective coloration required for his line of work.

Circling my hair I had pinned a shimmering choker necklace of Grandmother Bard's "big ol' diamonds," as she referred to them. It was a princessy touch, and I felt regal. I have always liked playing dress-up, and I was having a terrific time feeling like the dressing up effort had pleased the citizenry.

My favorite part of dressing up tonight had been playing naughty shoe store customer with Thorne as, before I'd put on my dress, he sat me on the edge of the bed and knelt to buckle the ankle straps of my sexy blue suede shoes. I had limited my attire to his favorite lace-topped thigh-highs, and he had not limited himself to buckling.

I yanked my attention back to the ballroom and took a deep breath to force the sudden blush out of my cheeks. We had not yet encountered Mater and if I glowed too visibly she would use her unerring antenna-power on us and say icky things.

As we S-curved our way through the tables to my mother's, I wiggled my fingers to her friends, Charlotte Swansdon and Ann Donner, who were standing near the dais talking with the mayor's wife. They smiled and waved back, and Ann blew me a kiss.

"Alexandra, dear, it was so good of you to come."

I turned and Mater was holding out her left hand to me. I took it in my right hand and we held onto each other briefly and let go.

We hand-hugged this way instead of embracing, and we air-kissed, two cheeks passing in the night, so that Mater wouldn't "get mussed."

"Mother, I don't believe you've met Mr. Ardall. Louisa Bard, Thorne Ardall. Thorne, my mother Louisa."

I may have emphasized the word "mother" a little strongly.

Thorne watched her to see what my mother would do, and when she extended a hand palm down, duchess-like, he took it by the fingertips and bent over as if to kiss it.

He did not actually touch lips to fingers, but his bow was an old-world gesture not lost on my mother, the practiced man-catcher. She lit up with a coquettishness I was all too familiar with.

"Alexandra has told me so much about you," Mater said, which was an astounding and bare-faced lie. And then, goddam it, she patted her hair, as if every dyed strand were not sternly epoxied into place by a full can of extra-hold AquaNet.

"Nothing she has told me about you could possibly convey how lovely you are," he said.

Thorne trots out this sort of flummery only when he deems it absolutely essential, and tonight he deemed it essential to flummerize.

I have never seen anyone simper before, and I didn't much care for what it looked like now, but there was no mistaking what Mater was doing, and simpering was precisely what it was.

Mater is fastidiously groomed at all times, this evening wearing a deceptively simple Armani midnight blue dress with exquisite fluidity in the drape of the skirt's fabric. Every movement caught and reflected glints of light in the sheen of the sanded silk.

She was wearing her emeralds, Mater being the sort of woman who had a sufficiency of emeralds to wear. But then, who was I to talk, with my big ol' diamond headdress?

"Are you here with Teddy tonight?" I asked her.

Teddy is a walker. Mater, currently unattached, availed herself of Teddy's services as an escort when required.

Asking my mother about Teddy was meant to

be unkind, and I decided I would consider feeling some self-reproach later, after Mater had stopped flirting with my boyfriend.

"What dear? Oh yes. Teddy is fetching me a little something from the bar." Mater answered my question while looking up at Thorne rather than at me.

Thorne turned to me. "May I bring you a little something?"

And I, who never drink spirits, said, "Yes please. That would be lovely. Whatever you're having."

Thorne excused himself, knowing that I would like him to leave me alone with my mother, although I would not enjoy *being* alone with my mother. She stared at his back, a look of longing combined with calculation in her eyes.

"Mother."

I touched her arm to capture her attention.

"Do you mind if we sit? While we have a moment I wonder if you found anything in your yearbook about Sharonna Rooney."

"He isn't what I expected."

She was gazing at Thorne as he threaded his way between the tables.

"He's never what anyone expects."

"Who are his people?"

Mater was reflexively seeking to qualify him according to her two primary criteria: family rank and financial wherewithal. In other words, did he attain social viability in the Louisa Bard realm.

"I'll let you ask him."

She probably imagined that my granting her such permission was to her advantage, and that her questioning would not prove to be a futile and frustrating experience.

But of course it would.

Holding onto the back of a chair to steady myself, I stepped between her and her view of Thorne as he waited in line at the bar. A down-turned mouth showing her annoyance, she shift-ed her gaze to me.

"While I have a moment with you now, please do pay attention. This is important. Sharonna Rooney. You were going to see what you could find out about her."

"I looked for her in my yearbook and she wasn't there. She must have graduated some years before I did."

Mater sounded abrupt, but that was nothing unusual.

"Who graduated before we did?" DeDe said, appearing beside us.

"Oh, nobody," Mater said.

"Sharonna Rooney," I told DeDe. "I know she went to Sacred Heart and I'm trying to learn more about her."

DeDe jerked her head back in repulsion.

"Oh no, not Loony Rooney! You remember her," she said to Mater. "She was a transfer from St. Bridget's when we were seniors."

So much for Mater's valiant attempt to knock half a decade or more off her age. But why would she lie about such an easily verified fact?

"Oh? I don't think I recall her."

"Yes, you do," DeDe said.

"We weren't very nice to her," DeDe explained to me. "We all wore uniforms, of course, but she never wore the right sort of blouse or shoes, and she kept to herself and wore white lipstick, so we decided she was a slut. I'm afraid we teased her rather unforgivably."

She looked at me and added, "Now that we know more about the effect of bullying, I hope we wouldn't do that if we were back in school today."

DeDe was the softest-hearted of my mother's friends, and I liked her the best of them.

Teddy arrived with Mater's Scotch-rocks and his own champagne cocktail, and we exchanged greetings. He wore a plum-colored satin cummerbund and bow tie with his impeccably tailored tux. In formalwear or street clothes, Teddy was always amusingly dapper.

"DeDe," I said, "may I talk to you when things quiet down after dinner? I'm very interested in learning anything you can remember about Sharonna Rooney."

"Of course, Alexandra. After dessert and the mayor's speech I'll get Charlotte and Ann and we'll put our heads together. But why do you want to know about her? That was all so long ago."

"A friend of mine had a recent run-in with her, and we're trying to sort things out in the aftermath."

"Of course, dear. I'll see you later then."

DeDe patted my arm and headed to her seat at the table running the length of the dais. On folding tray stands around the periphery of the room banquet waiters were setting down wide round trays loaded with dinner salads. It was time to sit and eat.

As soon as DeDe turned her back, I felt my mother's hand clamp onto my wrist. Astonished, I looked down at her hand and then up at her. Mater almost never touched me, and right now her grip was painful.

"Mother!"

She hissed at me, "Don't be stupid."

"Let go of me, please."

I kept my voice down and turned my wrist to break her hold. My mother had forgotten, so I was reminding her of the most important WASP commandment: "Thou Shalt Not Make A Scene."

"Alexandra Bard, you have always been one

for getting in the middle of something because you think you can fix it. You can't fix anything, really. People are awful and you never know it until it's too late."

I stared at her, speechless. I could not remember her ever speaking to me so urgently, and I had no idea what triggered this startling outburst.

Soundlessly, Thorne appeared to hand me my drink—a non-alcoholic Collins mix with lime—and it broke the spell.

I hate the feeling of being even a little tipsy and I get a headache before I feel the slightest bit festive from booze, so even though I was sure what my mother had just done was exactly why most people need a shot of whiskey, I was glad to take a long sip of the soft drink.

The band finished playing, and couples began working their way back to their assigned tables. Mater collected herself, gathered her guests, and directed them to the seats she wanted them to assume.

She sat her friend Marie's handsome husband George on her right and Thorne on her left. She sat me across the table from her, between Teddy, whom I enjoyed because he kept me laughing with amusing but not mean-spirited gossip during the salad and dessert courses, and, during the entrée, Mr. Eljer Wyandott, a gentleman in his eighties who was hard of hearing and who enlightened me at some length as to the fascinating secrets involved in making a fortune from aluminum siding.

Hint: the secret is volume.

I knew I would have a bruise encircling my wrist in the morning, and I would have no idea why my mother had suddenly and vociferously spoken as she had.

I also knew that if I asked her she would never tell me why. She would insist it had never happened.

≈11≈

After the salad and salmon and parfait and mayoral platitudes, table-hopping commenced. The band shifted from quiet dinnertime ballads into a sprightlier gear and couples stepped out onto the parquet floor to dance.

I looked around for DeDe and saw her waving me over to a table in the corner where she sat with Charlotte and Ann.

"Will you excuse me, please?" I said to Mater. "I want to catch up with DeDe."

"Of course dear."

She turned to Thorne and put her hand on his forearm, flashing her slender fingers with their emeralds and their French manicure.

"I'm afraid I must excuse myself as well," he said, and stood. "If I don't get a chance to say goodbye later, I want to thank you for including me in this lovely evening."

"Am I to be left here all by my lonesome?"

There were eight other people at her table, and yet Mater actually pouted at Thorne as she spoke. She wasn't exactly blurry from the two Scotches and three Chardonnays she had glugged down during the meal, but she was getting there.

"Come along, darling," said Teddy, who had missed none of Mater's coquettish hijinks during the meal. He stood and walked around the table to pull out my mother's chair for her.

"Time for us to trip the light fantastic. You know you love to waltz. If you will do me the honor."

Teddy bowed to her as he spoke.

She took Teddy's hand, but she turned to Thorne.

"Do you waltz, Mr. Ardall?"

"Doesn't everyone? But another night."

He took my hand.

Mater was visibly peeved, but there was nothing she could do about it, so she slipped her hand under Teddy's proffered elbow and they headed to the dance floor.

"You were very debonair with her during

dinner," I said, as we began walking toward De-De's table.

"Yes."

"Did she find you acceptable? With the Main Line pedigree and the Princeton and Harvard education?"

He stopped and turned us to face each other.

"Look at me."

I looked at him. My eyes may have been a little red and watery. He held me lightly, his big warm hands curved around my bare upper arms. Our eyes locked, my blue eyes and his dark green eyes. I could barely breathe.

"It's you, all you, no one but you. She got nothing from me. She doesn't know any other way to act and it's sad. Take a deep breath and let it go."

I took the requested deep breath and exhaled shakily. I'm not sure I let "it" go, but I stopped feeling the urge to scream and cry and throw crockery. And murder my mother. At least for that moment.

"Okay?" he said.

"Okay."

I felt my hurt and anger transform into rage at what had already happened to Netta, and might yet happen to her or others.

"Let's go talk to the ladies who admit to knowing the goddess way back when," I said, "and gather some facts about the formative years of her nasty self and whatever the fuck she's claiming to be the goddess of."

He extended his arm, and I clamped onto it in case any residual rage made my ankle as wobbly as my emotional state.

He steered me clear of the remaining crockery on the tables we passed. Better safe than sorry.

≈12≈

I introduced Thorne to Ann and Charlotte and they stared at him, just not as dedicatedly as many people are unable to avoid doing. They hugged me and held out their hands for him to shake, waving at empty chairs for us to avail ourselves of.

DeDe had rounded up three full bottles of white wine and the trio sipped steadily from their wine glasses as our conversation progressed. There were two clean glasses waiting in front of Thorne and me. Thorne left and returned with a full water pitcher and poured for us.

"The dinner was delicious, and this is a lovely

party," I said.

"But what you really came over for is to ask us to put our collective memories together and fill you in on Sharonna Rooney," Charlotte said, raising her glass in a toast and taking a sip of wine.

I smiled and shrugged.

"Yes, please, if you would."

"We've been comparing notes," said DeDe.

"We want to know more about why you're asking about her," Charlotte said.

She was wearing a red Valentino long-sleeved gown with tiers of knife-edge pleats cascading down the skirt, and she looked spectacular. Charlotte, with her mane of blonde hair, enjoys looking spectacular and has a knack for making spectacularity look like no effort at all was required.

"A friend of mine got into a bad scrape with her," I said.

"Well, that's no surprise," Charlotte said.

The ladies looked at each other and took a sip of wine. Apparently Ann was elected to kick off the debriefing.

"I can tell you she was definitely odd," she said. "We all thought so at the time."

Ann, with her neat cap of brown hair, was wearing a sleeveless black column sheath with floral embroidery on the bodice. The luminous silk embroidery was elaborate, hand-sewn, and must have taken hundreds of hours to stitch.

"We were high school girls," explained Charlotte. "You know how high school cliques can be. And it was a girls' private school, so the social setup was different from a coed public school."

"I think it's always the same," DeDe said, shaking her head. "High school girls can be really mean. And we were definitely mean to Sharonna."

She raised her eyebrows and lowered her chin at Charlotte and Ann, challenging them to argue with her.

"You have to admit she was strange," Ann said.

"How was she strange? DeDe mentioned the wrong blouse, keeping to herself, and wearing white lipstick. That stuff doesn't seem—to me anyway—like such a big deal. What else did she do?"

"She didn't keep entirely to herself," Charlotte said. "She gathered all the misfits to her like iron filings to a magnet, and she ran them around doing errands for her. She was a total queen bee when she could get away with it. And she dyed her hair black. It was mousy brown at the beginning of the year, and then she dyed it pitch black."

"This was before everybody went off and got into punk and goth and all that," DeDe added. "We didn't even know Elvis dyed his blond hair black until we were much older."

"I remember Sharonna dying her hair, but I don't remember her having a troupe of followers," Ann said.

"Charlotte is right," DeDe said. "We were in religious studies and we learned the word 'acolyte,' and after class we were talking by our lockers about how Sharonna had acolytes."

"That's right. I remember now. We laughed at the idea of it, that anybody would want to spend all her time controlling a little troupe of otherwise undesirable girls. Sharonna didn't seem boy-crazy like we were. But then that turned out not to be true."

My mind's eye jumped to the image of the High Priestess card, a subtle woman wearing a horned tiara and diaphanous blue robes, and holding a scroll, or sometimes a cup. What was in the cup? What mysteries did she hide, or reveal, in her secret religion?

Charlotte's voice pulled me back.

"Didn't Louisa have to fix her up for the prom?" she asked. "Because Sharonna's mother volunteered to host the after-party and the headmistress accepted before the rest of the class could stop it?"

"Oh that's right!" DeDe said. "And we all had to go!"

"She was tall, Sharonna was, over six feet.

Taller than the date Louisa found for her. I forget what Louisa had to do to convince him—I think he was her cousin, wasn't he?—to be fixed up," Charlotte said.

"That's right. It was Louisa's cousin Phil," Ann said, "and at the after-party didn't the two of them manage to get drunk or something? They were making out on the couch in the Rooney's downstairs rec room as if they didn't care if anyone else was there."

"*What?!*" said DeDe. "Were they really? Where was I when that was happening?"

"Was that so shocking?" I asked. "For a couple to make out on prom night?"

"The way they were going at it, yes," Ann said. "This was decades ago, remember, before it was easy to get the pill when you were in high school. Before everybody was giving blow jobs at the age of twelve."

"Can you imagine how naïve we were then?' DeDe laughed. "But even if it were nowadays, I still think it would be strange for a girl to be that, well, fast. To carry on like that with a blind date."

"DeDe, dear, you always were a very good girl." Ann patted DeDe's hand.

"Wasn't there something after the prom? Something about Louisa's cousin?" Charlotte asked.

The three women put their wine glasses down

on the table with three little thumps and began talking over each other, waving their hands up and down and pointing for emphasis.

"Yes!"

"That's right!"

"Oh my Lord! He died!"

"Yes!" Charlotte said to me. "We were all so shocked. And Louisa took it very hard."

"Wait a minute. Who died?"

"Louisa's cousin!" Charlotte said, and then looked back at Ann and DeDe. "Phil something. What was it? Phil Finneran! The cousin Louisa fixed up with Sharonna. He was a senior at Saint Ignatius."

"How did he die?" I asked.

"It wasn't made clear at the time, was it? Did you ever know what really happened?" Ann looked from Charlotte to DeDe and picked up her wine glass again to take a sip.

"I never did. When I asked my parents about it they got very close-mouthed," DeDe said, staring down at her near-empty glass and reaching for the wine bottle.

Thorne stood, picked up one of the open bottles, and the ladies lined their glasses up in a row on the tablecloth. He poured, they smiled at him and sipped, and he sat back down.

"It was all gossip," Charlotte said. "I know Phil and Sharonna were seeing each other for a little while after the prom because, if I remember correctly, Louisa made a comment one time. I think she said Phil wanted to break up but Sharonna was making trouble about it."

"That's right," Ann said. "I remember Louisa was not happy about the two of them dating. She only fixed them up in the first place because we ganged up on her to do it. We were down to the last minute and nobody could find Sharonna a date, and we knew Louisa could prevail upon Phil to go with Sharonna because Phil was Louisa's cousin."

"But what happened to him?" I said.

"It was a car fire, wasn't it?" Charlotte said. "I overheard my parents talking about it."

"Oh, yes. That's right, I remember now. It was awful," Ann said, grabbing Charlotte's arm. "His parents had given him a car for his eighteenth birthday and the police found him in it. From what I remember they thought he might have been passed out drunk and set himself on fire with a cigarette."

"Oh, how awful," DeDe said. "I don't think I ever knew this." She pressed her hand flat against her chest, over her heart, and shook her head in dismay.

"Everybody smoked back then," Charlotte said to me. "If I'm not mis-remembering, they found the car in the old tunnel that goes from the

Sausalito freeway exit through the hillside into the Marin Headlands. The car was burned out, with Phil still inside."

She looked to Ann and DeDe for confirmation.

"Please," DeDe begged. "No more. Now I don't blame my parents for never telling me what happened."

"Then Sharonna left school suddenly. Nobody ever knew why. She missed graduation." Ann looked to Charlotte for confirmation of her recollection.

"That's right. It was a week before graduation. I don't know if she got a diploma or what. Poof! She was just gone."

"There was gossip. There's always gossip when a girl leaves school suddenly," DeDe said.

Charlotte whispered, "That she was in trouble. That Phil had knocked her up. That Sharonna's parents did something to him."

They all nodded their heads.

"No wonder my mother is refusing to remember anything about it," I said. "If she feels responsible for getting Phil involved in the relationship, and thinks Sharonna was even slightly involved in Phil's death."

"Xana, honey..." Charlotte squeezed my hand. "Your mother thinks she controls the entire universe and everything and everyone in it. God is merely her personal assistant. She started acting like that right after Phil died. Not that she could ever manage to make it be true."

Ann and DeDe nodded their agreement.

"We all love her anyway," DeDe said, taking and squeezing my hand. "Lord only knows why, but we do."

And once more they all nodded like dashboard dolls, and took another sip of wine.

≈13≈

The next morning I paid the price for wearing the high heels. Vanity being an occasionally rewarding vice, I wasn't all that sorry about the pain my recovering ankle relayed reliably back and forth along my nervous system. It had felt so good to be out for an elegant evening, looking my best, squired by my imperturbable thug swain.

And undoing shirt studs and cufflinks is significantly sexier than undoing buttons, in my opinion. I have done the research.

Using the cane to keep me steady, I tucked the strappy blue suede heels back into their shoe box, stored it on the top shelf in the closet, and resolved to stick to flats for the remainder of my indeterminate recovery period. Cushy-soled flats.

Over "Eggs Ben Addiction" at Rose's café Thorne and I agreed that I would call DeLeon and check in. When DeLeon answered he said, "Can you come over now?"

So we drove over there now.

The Davies house was quiet at midday. I could smell that Maxine had baked something scrumptious, but then Maxine made sure the Davies house always smelled like something scrumptious.

Sunshine poured into the house from the sliding glass doors that led to the back yard.

Netta was nowhere to be seen.

DeLeon saw me looking around and said, "She's at the shrink's. We thought she maybe needed a chance to talk it through with somebody who wouldn't be gettin' emotional."

Maxine nodded agreement, and then said, "There's sweet potato pie."

She announced this as if sweet potato pie just occurred in the world, like dawn or snowstorms.

But then, in my world, it does.

"Anyway," Maxine said, leading us into her massive kitchen, "it's probably better that Netta isn't here to listen to us talking about her. She's torn up about what happened, all embarrassed about everything."

"Who's with her?" Thorne said.

"Terrell," DeLeon said. "One of us is always with her now, until this shit settles down. And thank you for checkin' in on things for the last couple of days."

I looked at Thorne. Of course he'd been checking in, while I, all self-absorbed, played dress-up, fiddling around with shoes and hairdos.

We were seated at the round table in the breakfast room, and I waited until the pause in the small talk. The pause was caused by the fact that all of us were gazing with well-deserved admiration at the beautiful pie Maxine had baked.

There was real whipped cream in a crystal bowl, with a large spoon tucked into it. I am extremely fond of whipped cream, and a large spoon should be the law of the land whenever and wherever whipped cream is present.

"You can tell me to mind my own business, and I probably should," I said as Maxine dished out servings. "We've learned some things since we went and got Netta back that you may find it helpful to know. And I'd like to be sure Netta has told you everything she told me."

Maxine took a crumpled tissue out of her pocket and held it to her nose. DeLeon reached for her free hand and held it. Thorne moved his chair closer to her and put his big hand on her shoulder.

"We could see that workin' in the field the way they made her do was tough on her," DeLeon said, "but that's not the worst thing they did. Netta told us about the young man who talked her into goin' to the farm in the first place.

"This guy Finn was supposedly a medical student at UCSF before he joined this cult. Netta said she had to fight him off pretty regular, once she got to the farm. She said he moved her from helpin' the cook to workin' in the field because of she wouldn't give in to him.

"And when Netta was sick to her stomach one morning he and that bitch goddess asked Netta a bunch of questions. Then they gave her a pill, they said for nausea. Two days later they gave her a 'vitamin.' She miscarried."

"But it wasn't a miscarriage," I said, remembering how Netta had sobbed over this part of her story the other night.

"No," DeLeon shook his head. "I know a lot of things can go wrong in a pregnancy. But they made sure my little girl would lose it."

I remembered the Princess of Cups card in the reading I had done before we headed to Marysville, and the flash of intuition I had had about Netta being pregnant.

I thought about the Four of Cups and its meaning: dissatisfaction with a situation and also with what is offered in its stead.

I wondered if Netta had thought, the way some young women do, that having a baby would somehow mend a relationship that was troubled, or provide love where love was missing.

I remembered the Five of Pentacles, with its self-imposed exile and feelings of unworthiness.

"The pregnancy is what you had the big fight about a few weeks ago, yes?" I asked Maxine.

She nodded.

"What would you have done if she had stayed here and stayed pregnant?"

"If she wanted to go through with it, then we'd have helped her," DeLeon said. "There are worse things in the world than an unexpected grandchild."

He smiled ruefully at me.

"I think she was afraid of what I would say. Or even do. She knew I didn't like her boyfriend."

He sighed.

"I know some parents go kickin' their kids out for misbehavior, and maybe she was afraid we would do that with her, or go after the boy. But if she wanted to have the baby or not, we'd have been okay with it either way. You get yourself into a bad situation like Netta did and you're old enough to have to face the consequences, I think you make a decision and your family has to find a way to deal with it. So if she decided to have the child, we'd have helped out so she could finish

school and get up on her feet. But those mother-
fuckers took the decision away from her, without
her even knowin'."

His volume rose and his voice wavered as he
finished speaking. Maxine was crying silently,
dabbing at her eyes with the tissue.

"Tell about the barn," she said.

I remembered what Netta told me about the
barn. I let DeLeon tell the story again. He shook
his head, looking down at his empty plate.

"You're not gonna believe this shit. I don't
know if I believe it. Netta said the first night after
she switched from cookin' to workin' in the field
she was sore and couldn't sleep. She got up to
scout around for some aspirin. She heard voices
outside and went to peek out the window and
there was a man had come to the farm, callin' out
for his sister.

"Netta said the man was out in the driveway
next to the house, shoutin' his sister's name. Netta
saw the boss woman and Finn run outside and
corral the man, takin' him by the arm. She heard
them tell the guy his sister was in the barn,
milkin'. You'd think any damn fool would know
you don't milk cows at midnight. Netta said they
went into the barn and shut the barn door, and
then a few minutes later Renenet and Finn came
out but the man did not. She saw Finn climb into
the man's car and drive it off somewhere.

"The next mornin' Netta asked Finn about it, sayin' she'd been woke up by the noise, and Finn told her the man had gone away. That he'd been mistaken about his sister bein' at the farm. But Netta said the man was callin' for Greta, and there was a woman named Greta sleepin' in the same dorm room with her."

"Did she ever find out if the man was still in the barn?"

"She had to go in there every mornin' to fetch the tools they used in the field. But the next day, 'cept for some hay bales moved around, there wasn't no sign of anythin' different from the day before."

I looked at Thorne.

"Cops?"

"No."

"Why not?' I was aghast. "We've got the forced abortion, the possible body in the barn, the kidnapping. Something needs to be done about this."

"She went up there willingly. She miscarried. She was dreaming."

"He's right, Xana," DeLeon said. "I think we have to let this go. We have to focus on helpin' Netta."

"Are you really going to insist on actual evidence instead of the word of a sixteen-year-old runaway?"

Thorne gave me his steady green stare. I let out a snort of frustration and turned to DeLeon.

"I haven't told you what we learned about Sharonna Rooney. Loony Rooney, the girls at Sacred Heart called her."

I related what I had learned at the gala the previous night. DeLeon and Maxine expressed no surprise at what I had heard from Sharonna's classmates.

"What difference does all that make now?" Maxine said.

I looked first at Thorne, and then at her.

"Winston Churchill once said, 'I like things to happen, and if they don't happen I like to make them happen,'" I said. "I love the old shit disturber for saying that. I think that if I see something that needs to be done, and nobody else is doing it, then it falls to me to step up and do it."

"Miz Xana, no," DeLeon said. "It is too dangerous. And no way is it your responsibility."

"I agree it is dangerous. We will spend our time assessing the danger and planning the best way to minimize it."

Thorne smiled his little smile. He likes hearing me think out loud the way he thinks inside his head.

"When I'm ready, when we've planned as carefully as we can plan, I'm going to go up to that farm and find a way to bring that woman and her creepy little toady pimp to justice."

I felt rather full of myself just then, self-righteous as well as severely codependent. I thought that if we all put our heads together we could figure out a way to come out on top in the end.

Then I remembered another quote, by Mark Twain: "Let us consider that we are all partially insane. It will explain us to each other."

≈14≈

Thorne and I spent two jam-packed weeks pre-paring. We worked all day, every day at hammer-ing out contingencies and perfecting our strategy and tactics and resources and skills.

I admit that it's my general inclination to go flying directly into the fray without any thought to planning or consequences.

"None of that tomfoolery," Thorne said, when I wanted to leap before looking.

To begin with, we sat down with Netta after she returned home from her therapist appoint-ment.

No, she had not seen any firearms anywhere while she was at the farm.

No, there was no secret basement room that she had ever spotted.

No, there were no drugs, to her knowledge. Everything was supposed to be natural; they used the horses rather than machinery for the heavy farm work like plowing and haying.

There was a dog to keep the rabbits and other vegetable-nibbling critters at bay, and some barn cats for the field mice, but no, there were no children, which I found odd, given the population of women, and then not odd at all, given what had been done to Netta.

I remembered that the High Priestess card was interpreted to imply a virgin moon goddess and potential, not actual, fruitfulness.

As our planning evolved, I started to put the preliminaries into action.

I went to the Goodwill store down at Civic Center and bought worn-looking oversized dresses in flower patterns, a man's leather bomber jacket, and a tired pair of leather hiking boots. I left the dresses hanging outside overnight to gather dust and moisture.

I let my hair grow past my regular salon appointment. I swabbed off my toenail and fingernail polish and stopped trimming my nails or cutting away the cuticles. I ceased waxing and went *au naturel*.

"Woodstock forever," in other words.

I went to Chinatown and bought a cheap red wheeled grocery cart, the kind that folds open with an upright wire basket sitting on two wheels. I sat at the workbench in the garage and banged it around with a lug wrench to chip off some color and generally get some usage faked onto it.

I bought a big bag of cheap dog kibble and put it into the basket, along with a metal bowl and the old clothes I had purchased, everything twist-tied into a dark green garbage bag.

I affixed decals and stickers to my shiny, hospital-issue cane and rubbed dirt into them, and then scraped at some of them with a scissors.

I bought a pair of unlined brown pigskin driving gloves, minus with the fingertips, and wore them everywhere to break them in.

I bought a cheap sun hat with a wide brim and a drape hanging off the edges to protect my shoulders and neck. I washed and bleached it a dozen times and left it out in the yard to fade.

Every morning I schooled Hawk, who would be my companion, on off-leash heel, sit, stay, down, come, and—most important—find Thorne.

We practiced "Find Thorne" at increasing distances. Hawk loved the game and grew adept at sniffing out and racing to the Manzilla holding the dog biscuit.

Hammering out contingencies, we realized

"Find Xana" would be equally as important a trick, so Hawk happily played that game, too.

I got a tetanus booster and took Hawk with me to the rent-a-horse stables on the dunes across the coast highway from the Olympic Club Golf Course, so that both of us could get comfortable working with and around the horses. Many years had passed since my jodhpur-clad riding lessons and I needed a different education for the farm up north.

Larry, the owner, taught me how to harness and hitch the horses to a wagon, and then drive the wagon to fetch hay from the barn. I mucked stalls to pay my tuition. Calmly and quietly, Hawk took to the horses like a born farm dog, but then he may actually be half pony, given his size.

Larry referred me on to a friend, Dave DeBiase, in Marin County. A pair of magnificent Percheron draft horses did the heavy farm work there, and I learned from Dave how to drive them using the right commands. Larry was happy to demonstrate and coach me in plowing and harrowing and haying skills.

Thorne called his bodyguard crony Don Madrone and under their tutelage I worked on identifying new ways to disable attackers. I couldn't easily balance on my left leg to kick with my right, and I couldn't generate a lot of power with my left foot when I stood on my right.

Krav-Maga teaches you to attack instantly and mercilessly the most vulnerable points on another person: groin, eyes, throat. Aikido teaches you to wield the attacker's power against him.

We spent time honing both disciplines, practicing a lot on fending off attacks with farm implements. As we did, I flashed back to the Eight of Wands card, with its image of eight wooden poles flying through the air.

So we added stick fighting to the regimen. I needed a cane for the time being, so I read A.C. Cunningham's book on using one as a weapon and then I practiced swatting, jabbing and hooking with mine.

Because I would be working with farm tools, I called Rose Sason's son Marco. He showed up each morning for a week, wearing a loose cotton shirt and drawstring pants, both black. His short black hair shone with reflected blue highlights in the sunshine that flooded the emptied dining room. We had laid down padded blue mats in order to use the room as a martial arts studio.

Compact, sturdy, very fast on his bare feet, Marco greeted me every morning with an open smile that seemed to carry the sunshine indoors with him. As soon as we stood on the mat, however, he traded the smile for a scowl of concentration and he was all professionalism.

Thorne sat in on the sessions. Marco was careful and exact about where I was to hold my arms, how I was to shift my weight from foot to foot, how to parry and swing and thrust with the long sticks.

When my ankle protested, I said nothing about it and kept on moving as Marco told me to. Thorne noticed, of course, because he notices everything, and he interceded when he saw I was in pain, telling Marco he needed to learn the techniques so he and I could continue to practice once Marco went home.

When Marco was satisfied that I could competently demonstrate the basics, he made the necessary adjustments to materials and technique to prepare me to fight using a hoe and a pitchfork.

In the meantime, DeLeon, via his high-tech industry contacts, procured a GPS transmitter that looked like a buckle and would fit onto Hawk's collar. It came with an unobtrusive miniature solar-powered charger that provided nonstop juice.

Long ago I taught Hawk not to accept food from strangers, and not to eat anything he found lying around. I made him practice and practice that unnatural restraint. He's a dog, though, and millennia of biochemical hard-wiring have gone into every dog's role as one of Earth's premier garbage recyclers. I would have to keep a close eye on him.

I slept well, night after exhausted night. I thought sleep would prove harder to come by when I reached the farm, but not because I was going to be any less exhausted at the end of a farm workday.

I was afraid I would give myself away somehow when I was unconscious.

And as a result of unconsciously giving myself away, get myself killed while I slept.

≈15≈

Three days before the planned departure date the doorbell rang. The dogs barked and ran downstairs to greet whoever was waiting to come in.

Zack and Wendell were waiting to come in.

They were each wearing jeans, T-shirts and hoodies. Zack's hoody bore the image of an X-wing star fighter and Wendell's was emblazoned with a crouched Spider-Man. Their hair, longish and tucked behind their ears, looked like it had not been invaded by shampoo anytime recently.

"DeLeon sent us," said Zack. "He's one of our venture capitalists. He's the awesomest dude."

They both looked to be about fourteen years old, but Thorne quietly assured me on the way down the hall to the kitchen, which was where they wanted to go, that they were highly compensated design engineers working at a Silicon Valley start-up, and were both MIT graduates with doctorates in something it was useless to describe to me, since I would neither understand the description, nor how it was they could earn so much money and not between them own a single clean T-shirt.

I took offense about the doctorate wisecrack, so I asked Zack and Wendell about their degrees. As near as I can tell they said something about studying how cosmic rays affect individual grains of sand, but that's pure guesswork on my part. They didn't actually say the word "anti-disestablishmentarianism," but some of the words they did say had almost as many syllables. I think. They might as well have been speaking Klingon for all the meaning I managed to take from their descriptions.

What I did grasp is that DeLeon and his ultra-nerd resources had come up with a solution for how I could stay in touch with Thorne, or call for his help, without carrying a cell phone.

"Why are you soaking my arm?" Wendell was pressing wet paper towels to my bicep.

Zack was unwrapping the smallish package he had carried inside.

"For a tattoo," said Wendell.

I jerked my arm away.

"I most certainly am *not* getting a tattoo for this little escapade. There are limits."

In that moment I realized with a flash of chagrin that I sounded exactly like my mother.

"It's temporary. It washes off in a couple of weeks," Wendell said.

"What do I need a tattoo for?"

"To hide your phone," Zack said.

I stared at Zack. I stared at Wendell. They grinned happily.

"This is going to be so awesome," Zack said. "We've only tried this in the lab until now."

He held up a flat plastic-wrapped item that fit into the palm of his hand.

"Really?" I said to Thorne.

He gave me one of his looks. I read it as "Courage," sighed, said farewell to my tranquil mind once again, and looked at the nerdy boys.

"Okay. Just please note that I am neither a rat nor a monkey."

"Just to be sure, you're right-handed, yes?" Zack said.

I lifted my right hand and wiggled my fingers.

"I was right. This goes on your left arm, then," Wendell said.

I sighed and held out my wet left arm again. I admit my arm was looking tan and toned these days from all the martial arts and stall-mucking and haying. It looked exactly the way you want an arm to look if there's going to be a prominent tattoo affixed to it.

And then I laughed as Zack held up the tattoo decal. It was an eight-inch-long snarling black panther. I would be sporting the graphic cousin of Meeka and Katana as I went on my journey for justice.

Once the tattoo decal had dried on my bicep, Zack showed me a transparent rectangular patch about the size of an extra-large Band-Aid. It was imprinted with the black-dotted outline of a phone's pushbutton face.

In his other hand he held up a small spray canister and aimed it at the middle of the fake tattoo.

"What is that?" I said.

"Liquid nitrogen."

He pressed the lever on the top of the canister. I jumped when an incredibly cold spray numbed my arm in the center of the tattoo.

"You have to hold very still now," Zack said, as Wendell handed him a miniature scalpel.

I looked at Thorne with my sad puppy look, wondering what the hell he had gotten me into by inviting these two kids to perform surgery on me—these two kids who appeared not yet old enough for their parents to permit them to handle sharp objects.

I felt pressure on my arm and looked down at it. Through the tiny incision he had made, Zack inserted a couple of eentsy tubes under my skin.

I found it really yucky and also really fascinating. I watched carefully while he and Wendell explained what they were doing, triggering the tubes to uncoil beneath my skin. Wendell applied a dot of Krazy Glue to the incision to seal it.

Then Zack touched the center of the high-tech black-dotted Band-Aid which was camouflaged by the tattoo and it lit up looking exactly like a phone keypad.

"Awesome!" they both yelled.

I can tell you that it is downright freaky to have a chunk of your upper arm light up.

"Okay," Zack said. "So we've installed a blood-powered cell phone. You turn it on and off by tapping the surface of it."

Wendell tapped the center of the illuminated rectangle and the phone faded into the tattoo.

"It's masked by the tattoo, so it's essentially invisible. It holds onto your arm the same way a lizard can hold onto a rock or the ceiling. You program it with voice commands."

They were very excited that it was working. They had a tough time keeping their voices from cracking into a falsetto.

"What about sweat?" I asked. "And showers?"

The dweeb team interrupted each other explaining about the exchange of blood and glycogen for energy to power the phone, and how the matrix of black-dot pixels did something very necessary, and how the lizard-grip feature would enable the phone to cling to my arm no matter what for a couple of weeks, until new skin cells made it slough off.

"Hang on, guys," I said. "I love that you love this thing. What I really need to focus on right now is how do I turn the phone on and off, how do I activate it to transmit conversations, how much antenna power does it have and, most importantly, how do I make the 'get me the hell out of here' phone call?"

Wendell walked me through storing the necessary voice commands, which were basically "Call Thorne," and "Call 911."

We set up a one-button code following the star key that would dial Thorne without my needing to speak. Zack and Wendell took turns coaching me until I could make a call in under three seconds.

I was assured by the lab wonks, who held their right hands up as if they were being sworn in as witnesses, that as long as my blood was flowing the phone would work just like a regular cell phone, and that—a really great feature—it would also alert me to any blood-related health problems like leukemia or diabetes.

I thanked the pixel twins and practiced some more at calling Thorne's phone from my arm. Damn if my panther tattoo didn't work exactly the way they said it would, time after time after time.

I gave Zack and Wendell oatmeal cookies and bottles of water for their drive back to Menlo Park.

I practiced some more on the unsettlingly biological puma-phone.

You know, I have to admit it was totally awesome.

≈*16*≈

I was as ready as I was going to get, given my fever to get going immediately and my prudent awareness that I had to wait until I was thoroughly prepared.

Thorne and I were sitting on the deck after dinner, bundled up in pants and jackets to watch the sun set into the ocean. It was late spring and the evening temperature was in the low sixties or thereabouts, but the evening wind off the ocean was as chilly as it always is. I was curled sideways on Thorne's lap, my shearling-shod feet tucked behind his knees, his arms wrapped around me.

"You don't have to do this," he said.

"'Take this cup from me, Lord?' I think my hand is gorilla-glued to this particular cup."

"We haven't talked about why."

So I paid some attention to why I wanted to do this lunatic thing. I thought about the compulsion I felt to devote my full attention to the role I intended to play in bringing Sharonna Rooney down.

I wondered where my compassion had fled to, in light of my usual willingness to give everyone the benefit of the doubt, even queen bee cult leaders.

"Part of it is the elation of having a purpose," I said.

"You are not your job."

"I get that. I am also not someone who sees abuse of power and ignores it."

"Is that what this is about?"

"No." I leaned away a little to look up at his face.

"It may very well be about something else entirely. It may be about the fact that Sharonna was possibly responsible for hurting my family. She was definitely responsible for hurting DeLeon's family, and probably many others. It may be that I am deranged enough to believe I have the capability of evaluating good versus evil and plunking myself squarely down on the side of goodness."

"A good girl." He smiled his minimal smile.

"More than just that, although being a good person is difficult enough to pull off in this world we live in."

"What else?"

"What I meant by 'having a purpose' is that feeling of being illuminated by some force that empowers me, that breeds greatness of soul, that triggers everything in me that is excellent, and infinite, and fearless. That demonstrates to me and everyone else who I really am."

Thorne tightened his arms around me and kissed the top of my head.

The sun dropped near the horizon, half burying itself in the marine layer of fog, the visible half glowing traffic-cone orange.

"I love sponsoring my third graders," I said, thinking about the nine- and ten-year-olds I visited every week and tutored and fed and bought school supplies for and encouraged.

"And I love my life now, with you."

I felt my throat closing with emotion. I reached up and took Thorne's face in my hands.

"And neither those kids nor you, as wonderful as you both are, is everything I need. You help me, you free me, but you are flying buttresses rather than the cathedral, if that makes any sense."

Thorne bent forward and hummed into my hair. Possibly I was making sense, despite the buttress comparison. Possibly not. The hum sounded neutral, I thought.

I talked to Thorne's jacket collar.

"I think I spent years focused on the external, and I became adept at managing stuff that was not me. When I saw the High Priestess card at the outset of this crazy escapade, I thought about what the card might mean for me, and I'm still thinking about it. I think she was pointing me toward the internal, the nameless connection we all have, whether we believe it or not, to what's greater than we are, to our spark of potential that isn't manifested or known when we're born."

He murmured into my hair. "Karma? Dharma? Destiny?'

I took my hands away from his face and looked up at him.

"All I know is that I'm lit up again, like a charged battery. Everything in me says I am doing the right thing. I know people can feel that way about awful stuff too. For instance, I think Sharonna probably imagines she's doing the right thing, preventing the women around her from having children or even having contact with any men other than the pitchfork-wielding pimp."

"Are you afraid?"

"Oh God yes."

He hugged me close to him, holding my head against his chest, his big hand warm on my cold ear.

"You can call if off any time."

"I know."

We watched the sun sink, a bright sliver on the upper rim of the fog.

"Are you ready?" Thorne said.

"I am."

The sun slipped below the fog. Long bright rays of white light fanned out across the evening sky. We stayed nestled on the deck, watching the stars come out.

I was a little afraid to find out what Thorne thought of my latest whirlwind obsession, but I looked up at him and asked anyway.

"We haven't talked about how you feel about my doing this. You've never questioned it."

His eyes changed, as if a clear film had lifted off of them and the real Thorne was inside there gazing steadily at me.

"Would you go after Sharonna anyway?"

"If I had to go after her minus the stupefying puissance of thyself?"

"Just so."

I thought about it.

"It would take me longer to figure out how to do it, and I would need a village to back me up instead of just your fine self. But yes, I'd go after her."

"Yes, thou wouldst. With thine own flavor of stupefying puissance."

He stroked my windblown hair away from my face and tucked it behind my ear.

I thought about what he was saying.

"Let me see if I get what you are implying. Who knows how people figure out who they really are? Some do, some don't. Some realize it and shy away from it, for any of a number of valid or bogus reasons. Some of us figure it out later in life, and rejoice in the awareness. I think I'm one of the late rejoicers."

"And here we are."

"Yes." I smiled at him. "And you are nobody's wage slave, any more than I am anybody's bitch. We each do what it is in our essential nature to do, and we do it with everything we've got."

Thorne smiled his little smile. "Just so. And I am the world's most fortunate man to have found you."

I kissed him, a smiling kiss.

I don't know why I worry about what he's thinking. I imagine that, like so many men, if he didn't want to be with a woman, he would be gone.

Like so many women, I always want to hear that he's happy to stay.

I waited for Orion to march up over the horizon with his sword and his dog, Sirius. I decided Orion would be my sponsor on this quest. I was embarking on it wielding my sword-cane and accompanied by my trusty dog Hawk.

I would invoke the power of all the galaxies and all the planets and the moon goddess herself, who whispers her secrets to the High Priestess, our unconscious, the secret self in all of us.

For now, though, it was time to go inside for the night.

I kissed Thorne again, and felt the strength of him as he pulled me close to him and held me tight.

"How do you feel about sex with a slightly fuzzy girl?"

"Woodstock forever. We'll put on a Richie Havens CD, get under the shower to recreate the nonstop rain. Skip the mud and the bad acid."

≈17≈

We were ready to go. Thorne more than ready; me finally ready.

I had donned one of the saggy, loose-fitting flowered frocks and had pulled on the scuffed boots.

I had smooshed clay hairdressing in to gunk up my clean hair.

I had traded Hawk's handsome leather leash for a length of blue nylon rope.

I looked in the mirror and saw a distressed woman who had no cash to spare.

I felt frayed around the edges from lack of sleep the previous night.

I had packed a travel-size jar of cold cream in lieu of my facialist-provided moisturizer, and that was going to be my only concession to a daily beauty routine. I could almost feel crow's feet and marionette-line jowls lusting to manifest themselves.

The doorbell rang.

The barking dogs ran down the stairs. I followed them and opened the front door.

Mater.

The dogs peeked around me at my unexpected visitor. I heard the cats scrambling up the stairway carpet runner to hunker underneath my bed on the third floor, as they always do when Mater shows up.

I longed to join them.

"Alexandra, what in God's name are you wearing?"

"Hello Mother. This is a surprise."

"May I come in, please?" She took a step forward.

I blocked her way.

"I'm afraid it's not a good time just now. You should have called first. I have an appointment and I was just leaving."

"You can't possibly mean to go anywhere dressed like that," she said, looking me up and down.

"Mother, I'm busy right now. You should

have called me and saved yourself the drive."

I had a white-knuckle grip on the inside door-knob. It took all my self-control not to shout at her to go away and never come back, and then slam the door in her face.

But Mater had, as is her wont, parked her Cadillac sedan across my driveway and therefore blocked in my packed-up Chrysler. Blocking a driveway is, in the parking hell that is San Francisco, a Class C felony.

And then she astounded me. My mother, who never touches me if she can avoid doing so, reached forward and took my free hand in hers, her grip tight and unrelenting.

"Please, Alexandra. I am asking you to let me in. I need very much to speak with you. I didn't call first because I considered that you might hang up rather than talk. But I need to speak with you right away. If it were not urgent I would not have driven all this way to see you. Please hear me out."

The drive from Pebble Beach took her two hours, plus she's my mother, plus she actually said "please," so I stood aside and waved her inside. The dogs bolted upstairs ahead of her.

"Go to bed," I instructed them, as I trailed my mother's St. John suit and Ferragamos up the steps.

The dogs obediently curled up on their cushions in the foyer alcove.

I know Mater couldn't have heard it, because I didn't hear it, but I was confident Thorne had escaped down the outside stairway from the kitchen to the ground floor.

Her emeralds are actually kryptonite, I've concluded, and it had been an act of physical valor for my personal Superman to escort me to the black tie dinner.

"Would you like some coffee or tea? Or a glass of water?" I was thinking, *Please say no.*

"Nothing, dear, thank you."

Mater may be a world-class narcissist, but she is not dim-witted and she was not going to treat this like a social visit.

"May I?" she said, indicating one of the wing chairs.

"Of course."

She sat on the front edge of the chair seat, her back straight, her hands folded in her lap, knees pressed together, ankles crossed and tucked away under the chair.

I sat on the loveseat and faced her.

"Alexandra, you mustn't do this."

"Do what?"

I knew very well that she knew exactly what. Special agents in the junipers; it had to be.

"Collin called me," she said.

Collin is one of my two older brothers. He

lives with his boyfriend in Santa Monica, and I had called and told him my plan, just in case. I had sworn him to secrecy. I had specifically made him swear not to tell Mater.

Whoever said, "You can't get blood from a turnip" never permitted the turnip to make the acquaintance of my mother. But I've had enough psychotherapy to wonder whether I had in fact imparted my secret to Collin, trusting that he would relay it to Mater.

"I forbid you to do this," my mother said.

I have learned a life skill during my many years of therapy. That life skill is to ask a question instead of slapping someone in the face, even someone who presumes to forbid me to do what I damn well please now that I am a full-grown woman who has not borrowed any money from my mother recently.

So I used my hard-earned skill and asked Mater a question.

"Why do you think I should not do what Collin told you I was planning to do?"

"Because Sharonna Rooney is a murderer, and I don't want to lose another family member to her."

My mother paused, and then she astounded me again.

She said, "I don't want to lose someone I love again," and then she began to weep.

I have never seen my mother relinquish her emotional poise. Even squiffed, as she would phrase it, she may become revoltingly kittenish, but never maudlin.

Seeing the tears tumble down her carefully made-up face shocked me so thoroughly that I did what a normal person would do under similar circumstances: I went to her. I sat on the arm of her chair and held her while she cried.

I let go of her when she had recovered sufficiently to open her purse and pull out an embroidered cotton hanky, but I left one hand resting lightly on her back.

"Tell me."

As I had with Netta, I sat to Mater's side so we did not make eye contact.

"Did the girls tell you about my cousin Phil?"

She meant Ann and DeDe and Charlotte. She was pressing the handkerchief to her nose and under her eyes, careful not to rub her mascara as she collected herself.

"Not everything."

"How could they tell you everything? They don't know everything."

She pressed the folded hanky one more time to her nostrils and dropped her hand back to her lap.

"He was no relation, actually. We said he was my cousin but he was really my uncle's stepson.

His mother married my uncle Declan. We never met until we were both in high school. His mother was widowed when her first husband, who was rich in oil or some such, passed away"

She was still Mater. She was compelled to detail his background for me. And then she surprised me yet again.

"I loved him from the moment I saw him," she said, her voice husky with wistful regret.

"He was all I ever wanted, and I have never loved another man as I loved him. When Sharonna killed him she might as well have killed me."

I could barely hear her now. The rigor, the self-discipline, the ramrod spine of my mother— all were subdued into whispering misery.

"What happened?"

"They forced me to fix him up with her for the prom. I didn't want to. To this day I don't know why I agreed to do it. Phil didn't know I had a crush on him, you see, and I was afraid to ask him to go with me. He had never asked me out, and I thought it would look like I couldn't get a real date, you know, if I had to take my cousin. We were all so strict with our stupid rules about what was cool and what was not cool. So I asked Brian Morrissey instead. He was tall and handsome, and he'd asked me out once or twice so I knew he'd say yes, but he was nobody special to me. I thought our prom picture would look nice."

She was finding her way back to herself. She was talking about using other people to her own ends.

"And then?"

"And then Sharonna engulfed Phil. It was as if she drugged Phil with sex. My family had a Memorial Day party and he had the sense not to invite her, because any time they were together Sharonna was draped all over him and I think he was mortified by it. At the party I worked up the nerve to ask him about Sharonna. I will never forget what he said to me that night."

She picked up the hanky and held it to her eyes.

"Tell me."

"He said, 'Why didn't you ask me to the prom yourself? It was you I wanted to go with.'"

And Louisa, my tiger mother, burst into wailing tears. I held her again, and rocked her gently back and forth, and waited until the tears dried up.

"That night he told me he was going to break up with Sharonna," she said, between shuddering sobs. "He told me he was finished with her. We made plans to spend the summer together."

Mater sighed and shook her head, gathering herself again. She smoothed her perfectly flat knit skirt as she spoke, the diamonds in her ring and wristwatch glinting as her hand moved.

"We talked and talked all that evening. We sat out in the garden, after everyone had gone home, and we told our dreams to the full moon passing overhead. When I said that Orion was my favorite constellation Phil said to me, 'He's yours. I give you Orion, the Moon's beloved.'"

I had always loved Orion, since my mother first pointed the constellation out to me one night when I was a teenager.

"He watches over you for me," she said to me when I headed out the door on my first real date, "so be good."

That my aloof mother would assign a protector to me, even one whose duties were meant to include protecting me from any sexual adventure with the boy I was then enamored of, seemed like a loving act at the time.

There were few enough loving acts to compare it to, so I cherished it. Now I understood why Orion had been my designated paladin.

"Phil sounds like a sweet young man," I said.

"He was. He was. And that goddam bitch Sharonna killed him rather than let him go."

My mother curses so rarely that when she does, the curse words have the impact they're intended to have.

"How do you know that?"

"Phil called me and said he was taking her to the tunnel in the Marin Headlands. That it was where he always took her. That a gentleman told a girl he was breaking up with her in person rather than on the phone. I pleaded with him not to. I warned him Sharonna was not completely right in the head, that I was worried she would do something physically dangerous if she heard any news she didn't like. Phil refused to believe me. But I was right. I never saw him again."

"Charlotte said there was an empty bottle of booze in the car. That the police concluded he had gotten drunk and accidentally set himself on fire."

"*No!*" My mother twisted around to look me in the eye and gripped my hand.

"Phil did not like to drink. He would have a beer once in a while, but he never got drunk like so many other boys did. And he never smoked in his new car. It was a red Mustang. He treasured that car. It was his precious baby. No one was allowed to eat or drink or smoke in that car."

"Did you tell anyone about your suspicions at the time?"

My mother let go of my hand and turned away. I felt her sinking into despondency.

"No, I did not."

"Why not?"

"Because Sharonna came to my doorstep the morning Phil was found dead. She looked a wreck. She had walked across the Golden Gate Bridge, all the way to our house in Pacific

Heights, after setting him on fire. The reek of the fire was on her still.

"Sharonna told me that if I said anything against her, that if I told anyone that she had been with Phil that night, she would accuse my father of seducing her. That she was pregnant, and she would say my father was the reason. That she would make a scandal."

"But that was a lie."

"Yes, Alexandra, it was a lie. If she was pregnant, it was undoubtedly Phil's doing. But in those days, and it's the same now, accusing someone of sexual misconduct was enough to blacken his reputation forever. It doesn't matter in the least if the accusations are baseless. They stick to the accused forever, and they ruin his life.

"I knew Sharonna would do exactly what she threatened, and I couldn't allow that to happen to my family. So I was silent. And I have lived with the shame and despair of my silence every single day since then."

"Until now," I said.

"Yes. Until now."

She turned and took my hand in hers again.

"Because I will not lose you to her. She is a monster, and I refuse to lose you to her. I have lost enough."

Well, there she was again. This was once more all about Mater. And her saying that sentence was what it took to rattle me free of my empathy with her.

"Mother, she has to be stopped."

"But you do not have to be the one to do it."

"No, I don't. But she has harmed your cousin and you, and she has harmed my friend DeLeon and his daughter Netta. She has perhaps harmed many more people who are not my friends, but who deserve justice. So I am going to make her pay."

Mater's tone changed to agitated insistence.

"She is *ruthless*. She is *insane*. She has no doubt fashioned herself into some kind of queen bee again. She will have surrounded herself with people who do whatever she bids them to do."

"Mother, look at me, please."

I knelt in front of her and took her hands in mine.

"Please, please see me as I am now," I said.

I waited until she made eye contact with me.

"I am strong. I am loved. I am competent. I am brave. I am smart. I trust in God and I am taken care of, every single day."

I held her gaze.

"I need you to see me that way. I need you to let go of the family myths about me, that I'm naïve and depressed and hapless. I am not those things. I can and will find the way to bring Sharonna to a reckoning."

Mater did not look away or emit her usual dismissive harumph, but I could see she remained unconvinced, so I made the decision to keep going.

"Do you remember Claudio?" I asked.

"How could anyone forget him?"

Now she was dismissive. She had never cared for Claudio. He was brilliant, and a poet, and hilarious.

But he was not rich, and his father worked as an orderly at Laguna Honda Hospital, San Francisco's county-operated old folk's home.

"He helped me see myself as I am for the first time," I said.

Claudio was born in Chile, and enjoyed amusing Americans with his Ricky Ricardo accent. He had been one of my wounded-bird projects, and in recompense he had helped midwife me into my adulthood.

"He said to me once, 'Ju need a rahbeet.'"

"What on earth? A rabbit?"

"Claudio said to me, 'Ju are a beautifool greyhoun', sleepin' in a sunny spot. Ju keep an eye open, always takin' a leetle peek, just in case a rahbeet come by. Ju quiet, *tranquila*, ju takin' a leetle nap, ju stayin' warm in the sun. But when a rahbeet come by—Whooosh! Ju off like a rocket. And ju gonna catch *el cornejo*, ev'ry time.'"

I smiled at my mother.

"I've seen a rabbit," I said, "and I'm going to go 'whoosh!'"

My mother looked at me steadily. I saw something shift behind her brown eyes.

"All right," she said. "All right. I do not like it one bit but all right. I recognize that look of yours, and I know you will not be stopped once you set your mind to something."

She shook her head in frustrated acquiescence.

"But you tell that tight-lipped colossus who is skulking around downstairs that if anything happens to you I will see to it that he is ground up into mincemeat and served *al fresco* to the coyotes of Big Sur."

And then I surprised myself. I hugged my mother, a real hug, and said, "Thank you for telling me this story. Thank you for worrying about me. Thank you for saying you love me."

And I kissed her, not an air-kiss but a real one, on her make-up streaked face.

"I have to freshen up this instant," she said, waving her hanky-filled hand back and forth to shoo me away from her. "I am quite certain I look an absolute fright."

≈18≈

Thorne drove. We were silent most of the way. Hawk was stretched out snoring on a dog blanket across the back seat.

As we exited north off Interstate 80 at Sacramento the image of the Princess of Cups card arose in my mind.

In the snapshot reading I had done before we rescued Netta, the card had been reversed. Now, when I saw it again, the word "heartbreak" came to me.

I thought of all the heartbreak that had surfaced during this adventure: Netta's, my mother's, even Sharonna's when Phil had dumped her after impregnating her.

Since in any reading the cards have something to tell me as well, I thought of the heartbreak I had gone through—the losses, the grief, the tears and loneliness and self-recrimination, the fear of taking emotional risks.

How is it that we recover? In what unexpected outbursts does grief manifest itself? How do we learn compassion for—and patience with—ourselves and others who are grieving? How do we come to trust that time will make a difference, will heal the heartbreak even if the memory of it may return without warning in a sharp twinge of sorrow and remorse?

Why do some people grieve for longer than others? Why is it that in some people heartbreak hardens into miserliness, cold-heartedness, vindictiveness, a need to manipulate others?

Or, as it did in me, morph into the need to hide out from life and refuse to run the risk of more pain? The High Priestess asks us to be open to our unconscious selves, to welcome our intuitions, to accept that inspiration and guidance will always be available to us.

She asks us to trust that, while some things will always remain unknowable, we are always connected to everything else in the universe. We are never alone.

No. If we feel alone it is because we have chosen to isolate ourselves.

I had allowed Thorne into my life, in spite of my misgivings, my pitiful romantic history, my self-doubt. I had allowed it because it was more important to me to remain open to the possibility of happiness than it was to shield myself from unhappiness.

I kissed my fingers, reached across the center console and touched my fingertips to his cheek.

He smiled his little smile, took his hand off the steering wheel to take hold of my hand, and kissed my fingers in return.

♪♪♪

Thorne pulled over just past the housing development east of Marysville, out of sight of the farm.

I climbed out of the car and opened the rear door to let Hawk hop down from the back seat. He stretched languidly and then looked around, sniffing the unfamiliar rural scents.

I pulled the wheeled basket from the trunk, took out my curtained sunhat, and tucked my hair up into it. I folded up the dog blanket and piled it on top of the other contents of the cart.

If people drove by us, I would look like a hitchhiker being dropped off.

As if anyone hitchhikes anymore.

"You won't see me," Thorne said.

"I know."

We looked at each other and exchanged a silent goodbye.

I tied the dog to his blue nylon rope, tied the rope to the handle of the wheeled cart, took my cane in my left hand, and began to walk. Thorne made a U-turn and drove back toward town.

The weather was San Joaquin Valley glorious: sunny, hot, clear, dry. Since it was late spring in California, there was virtually no chance of rain.

The shoulder of the road was level, so walking was easy enough. I gave Hawk a little extra rope-leash so he could avail himself of the weeds growing alongside the gravel.

I rounded a turn in the highway. A hundred yards ahead was the roadside stand for Renenet Farm. I stopped walking and stared at it. Cars and pickup trucks pulled in and out of the vegetable stand's parking area.

I saw the Seven of Cups card again in my mind. I reminded myself of its meaning: temptation to do something new, something captivating but unknown and potentially risky.

The hope and optimism and energy that arose whenever I embarked on any new undertaking had created a momentum that could mislead me, could cause me to blunder into something dangerous and rash.

And here I stood, on the verge of blundering into something dangerous and rash.

I wrestled my mind into a semblance of tranquility, shortened Hawk's leash, and kept walking, slowly and steadily, until I turned into the farm's driveway.

Midway down the driveway I pulled up my loose, elbow-length left sleeve and activated the blood-powered phone. It lit up, but in the bright sunlight the phone's glow was barely discernible.

"Call Thorne," I said, and let my sleeve drop. I talked to myself quietly, describing what I was seeing.

I knew Thorne was back toward town at the next farm over. He had rented a fallow field from the farmer and was pitching a solar-powered tent to occupy for the duration.

From the tent he would be able to track me by GPS and hear me by phone. His phone would be muted so nobody, including me, could hear him unless he wanted to be heard. He could see me in the binoculars if I was outdoors, and swoop in to fetch me if I got into trouble.

I was going to do my best to avoid getting into trouble. My plan for avoiding trouble was to act as dim-witted, and therefore harmless-seeming, as possible.

I walked straight to the twenty-yard-square

horse corral, rested my forearms on the top railing, and spoke to the big Shires. I clucked my tongue to call them over to me.

I reached into my pocket for the mini-carrots I had stashed there and held them out between the corral railings, one in the open palm of each hand, for the matched black mare and gelding to nibble into their mouths. As soon as they saw the carrots they trotted over to me.

Their manes were unbrushed, as were their tails and the white hair feathering around their hooves. Someone was not taking proper care of these beautiful animals.

I could see a chafed spot on the right shoulder of the mare, and a matching chafed spot on the left shoulder of the gelding. The gelding was almost a hand taller than the mare, which I figured meant he was the right-hand horse in the pair, and his job was to place one hoof directly in front of the other in the previously plowed furrow while the mare walked on the left, on higher unplowed ground.

"Hey!" called a tenor voice behind me.

I ignored the voice and continued to talk quietly to the horses, rubbing them under their chins. It was a man's voice shouting. I thought it must be Finn.

"Hey! Get away from those horses!"

The peremptory voice was closer now. I kept

talking to the big horses, my face close to their nostrils so we could exchange breaths.

Hawk bristled and growled.

"Sit," I said.

Hawk sat, facing the approaching man, and grumbled.

"I'll brush you," I said to the horses when I thought the man was close enough to hear me. "I'll fix your harness."

"Hey! I'm talking to you!" he said, standing back from the dog.

Hawk stood up and put his ears back.

"You need to get off the property. Right now."

I turned slightly so the man could see my face around the edge of my hat's drape. I didn't make eye contact.

He was thirty-ish, trim, maybe five-foot-ten or eleven, clean-shaven, with dark red hair and freckled skin. He wore a blue work shirt rolled up at the sleeves, black jeans, and black work boots.

I spoke quietly, in a monotone.

"They need brushing. A good brushing. They're rubbing each other's shoulders. It's not good for them. They're not happy. I can brush them. I can fix the harness so they don't rub shoulders. They'll plow better. They'll be happier."

I was speaking slowly, looking at the ground.

He studied me.

"Who are you?"

"Sandy," I said, after waiting a second or two.

"Sandy who?"

Again, I waited before answering.

"People call me Sandy."

"How did you get here?"

Pause. "Walking."

"From where?"

Pause. "There." I pointed back toward Marysville.

"Do you live there?"

I didn't answer.

"Where do you live?"

I didn't answer.

"Where is your home?"

Pause. "People let me help them. I help people. I help with horses."

He thought for a moment.

"Come with me."

I stood where I was.

"I want you to meet someone," he said, walking back and gesturing to me when I didn't follow him. "She'll decide whether you can help with the horses or not."

I stayed where I was.

"I want to brush the horses," I said, when he gestured again. "They're not happy."

He looked at me. I didn't look at him. We waited.

"Stay here. Don't do anything with the horses."

He turned and walked to the back door of the farmhouse, opened it and went inside.

"He's in the farmhouse," I said to nobody I could see.

I turned back to the horses and talked to them some more. To keep them near me, I pulled out two more carrots and fed them again.

Time went by. The sun was hot on my head. Hawk began to pant. A screen door creaked and slapped shut. I heard Hawk's muttering growl and continued to talk quietly to the horses.

"I'm going to get you a brush and we'll see, okay?" Finn had returned with instructions.

I waited, then turned slightly, without making eye contact.

"I'll brush them," I said.

Finn walked to the side door of the barn and swung it open. I saw a hay-strewn floor for the few feet inside the barn that the sun illuminated.

"He's gone into the barn," I said.

The man came back out holding a tired, dirty horse brush.

Hawk grumbled.

"I'm Finn."

He held the brush out to me at what he thought was a safe distance from the dog.

I waited a moment.

"Stay," I said.

Hawk stayed.

I walked to Finn to take the brush, looking at the brush the entire time. I took it out of his open hand and studied it.

"Where is water? I need water. And where is the harness? I need to fix the harness."

"What's wrong with the harness?"

Finn sounded annoyed. I had the sudden impression that he was the one responsible for harnessing the horses.

Pause. "The straps are too short. The straps."

"What straps?"

Pause. "The collar straps. The straps on their collars. They go between the collars and the bridles."

Horses plowing in a pair often have rings on the sides of their horse collars and bridles. A leather strap clips onto the ring on one horse's bridle and connects it to the ring on the other horse's collar, and vice versa, in an X.

The criss-crossed straps from one cheek to the other shoulder keep the horses perfectly parallel to each other. I was counting on this type of harness here, because of the visible chafing of the horses' hides.

"How do you know the strap is too short?"

Pause. "Look at his shoulder." I pointed. "Look at her shoulder. These horses grew.

They're Shire horses. They're big and strong. They grew."

"Are you saying the straps were okay when they were younger but now that they're full-grown the straps aren't long enough?"

I waited. I pointed at their mare's shoulder.

"They grew."

Thorne would probably be calling me "Rain Man" from this day forward, asking if it was time for Judge Wapner yet.

Finn looked at me.

I looked at the horse brush and began to pick dirty horsehair out of it.

"Where is water?" I said. "I need water."

"There's a spigot next to the barn door. Do you see it?" He was pointing.

Pause. "Yes."

I reached over the corral railing to grab a bucket that was hanging empty in the corner.

"Will the dog behave?" he said.

Pause. "Hawk likes horses. Horses like Hawk."

"Hawk? Why is his name Hawk?"

I waited. I held out my arms.

"He flies."

Finn looked at the dog. Hawk watched Finn closely, the dog's mouth open and panting, his tongue with each breath sliding in and out between two imposing lower canine teeth.

"When you're finished, come to the back door of the farmhouse and we'll get you something to eat," Finn said, eyeing me speculatively.

"I'm going to brush the horses." I walked with the bucket to the barn. "They need to be brushed."

Finn waited and watched as I filled the bucket with water and set it down. I washed the brush as well as I could and clawed the remaining horse-hair out of it.

I counterbalanced as I carried the heavy bucket back to the corral, the brush tucked into my pocket and my cane supporting my left leg as I walked.

I brought the sloshing bucket to Hawk so he could drink. When he stopped lapping at the water, I untied his blue rope and told him to lie down and stay.

I opened the corral gate and went in. The horses ambled over to me, their ears higher than mine by two feet. I gave them each another carrot and let them sniff the horse brush. I hooked my cane over the railing.

Finn climbed up and perched a few feet from my cane, watching me.

With Hawk's blue rope knotted through the tie ring of the gelding's halter I anchored the horse to the corral.

I began to brush the massive animal. I worked

gently on his snarled leg hair with the water and the brush to untangle it. Muck and straw peeled out of the feathery hair around his fetlocks and the hair whitened as I washed and brushed it.

When the long hair was clean and loose he stood placidly, barely shifting, as I began bringing up the sheen on his black coat. With each stroke of the brush, dust billowed off his hide.

"What's your name?" I asked the horse. "You're a nice boy, you're a good horse."

"Seth," said Finn. "The one you're brushing is Seth. The other horse is Blossom."

"Seth," I said after a moment, brushing the gelding's flank. "Blossom."

I picked up Seth's hooves one by one as I worked, checking them. They needed cleaning and filing, but it could wait for now; there were no abscesses or anything else that would cause immediate lameness.

"What's with the cane?"

Pause. "For walking."

"Did you always need a cane to walk?"

I didn't answer. I could feel his eyes on me as I worked.

I had to stretch on tiptoe the get to the top of the horse's mane. Finn was watching me closely as I moved around the animals, bending over and stretching upward, tending to the neglected draft horses the way someone else should have been doing all along.

I talked to Seth quietly as I worked, telling him he was beautiful and a good horse.

"You're very pretty, for a retard," Finn muttered.

I pretended not to hear.

"Come to the farmhouse when you're done."

He spoke more audibly this time, and swiveled to hop down into the barnyard.

I waited a moment. "Yes." I spoke to his back as he walked away.

≈19≈

I worked for more than an hour brushing the horses until their manes, tails, hooves, and hides were gleaming and clean. I risked going into the barn to find more hay, some grain, and a hoof pick. I spotted a rasp and a manure shovel and brought them along too.

I saw nothing in the barn that raised an alarm. There were two milk cows in stalls, stacks of hay, an array of farm equipment including a riding plow, a toothed harrow, a hay mower and rake, and other items a horse-powered farmer would use to plant and reap crops.

In the tack room I found a jumble of unkempt bridles, collars, and the harnesses the horses would use for their work on the farm. I could track down some neatsfoot oil later to clean and restore the dry leather.

I found the too-short harness straps and determined that with an awl I could punch holes a couple of inches closer to the clip at each end and move the existing rivets into the new holes. Adding another four or five inches between the horses when they were harnessed together would likely be enough to stop them from rubbing shoulders and hips.

When I returned to the corral, the farm dog Netta had mentioned was there investigating the newcomers. Hawk had gotten to his feet to assert his undeniable dominance. The farm dog, a terrier mix, was on her back, her paws in the air, her tail brushing the dirt back and forth in submission as Hawk sniffed her.

She was filthy. She couldn't be an indoor dog with her fur as matted as hers was; indoor dogs are for petting and nobody would want to touch this dog's fur.

There were foxtails and burrs caught in her paws, so I called her to me, fed her a few pieces of Hawk's kibble, and tied her to the railing.

I sat on the overturned bucket and cleaned and brushed her. She nibbled at and licked my fingers when I pulled a particularly painful burr out from between her footpads, but otherwise she sat placidly and allowed me to help her.

Hawk paid close attention to how much attention I was giving the other dog. Sometimes he
poked his big bony head in between mine and the
paw I was working on. Between us we persevered
in removing the burrs from between her pads.

When the dog was as cleaned up as I could
get her without giving her a long bath, I gave her
some more kibble, untied her, and she scampered
away.

I cleaned the horses' corral, carrying the shov-
elfuls of manure to the big pile that was accumu-
lating next to the one with the tarp and car tires.

By the time I had fed the horses, tended to
their hooves with the pick and rasp, and dumped
and refilled their water trough, it was four o'clock
or so, I figured.

I returned the tools and tack to the barn where
I'd found them, hung up the bucket on the corral
railing, peeled off my fingerless gloves, and spent
five minutes rubbing my hands and face in the
cold water coming out of the barn spigot.

I couldn't postpone it any longer. I jammed
the gloves into my pocket, gathered my cane and
cart, re-leashed my dog, and walked to the back
door of the farmhouse.

"I'm going to the house now," I said to my left
arm.

"Check," I heard back, my bicep speaking in a

deep baritone. He had to be watching in the binoculars, or he wouldn't have risked talking to me.

A deep screened porch ran from one side to
the other across the rear of the farmhouse. There
was no one on the porch. I opened the screen door
and went in.

A heavy Dutch door was half-open ahead of
me. The folded-back upper half of the door was
divided into glass panes.

Stepping out of the hot sun into the shade of
the house was a relief. The skin on my bare forearms was tight and pink from the afternoon spent
outside in the sun.

I stood waiting at the half door, looking into
the big empty kitchen. Piles of carrots, peapods,
yellow and green string beans, potatoes, Romaine
lettuce and red onions lay on the counters and on
a wide rectangular chopping block in the center of
the room.

Over the chopping block frying pans, stock
pots and cauldrons with handles hung from ceiling hooks.

I smelled bread baking. Bundles of rosemary
and other herbs hung drying above the refrigerator. A long braid of garlic was suspended from
the cabinet next to the sink.

I knocked, not very loudly, on the door frame
and then stood and waited. Someone would come
into the kitchen soon; the vegetables had to be

peeled and shelled and chopped for dinner. Hawk sat patiently at my side.

A plump gray-blonde woman with pink cheeks and bright blue eyes—sixty or so she seemed to be —limped into the kitchen from the opposite side. Her long hair swung in a thick braid down her back, and she wore a white short-sleeved blouse and Mom jeans.

In a practiced movement she reached for a blue-checked apron from a hook by the door and lifted the apron's neck loop over her head. Tying the strings behind her back, she looked up and saw me.

I averted my eyes.

"Well hello, hon," she said. "What are you do-ing there? You come right on inside and set for a spell, why don't you?"

She pulled open the half door, saw Hawk, opened her mouth in shock and stepped back, putting her hands up to her mouth.

The loose skin on her face was a soft gauze of wrinkles and her hands were age-spotted, with lumpy arthritic knuckles.

"My my, you're a big boy, aren't you?' She was not at all sure about the dog.

Pause. "I finished brushing the horses. The man told me to come to the house."

"Finn told you that?' She was still watching Hawk.

"I brushed the horses."

I put my hand on Hawk's head and stroked it, rubbing him behind the ears.

"You want to wait there on the porch, hon? Or you can come inside, but your friend has to stay outside."

I waited a moment.

"My shoes are dirty."

"Well, I want to know your Momma, who raised you so well." She smiled at me. "You can just leave off those dirty boots outside the door there."

I thought how very little this kindly woman would actually enjoy meeting my Momma.

I slipped off my boots and stood in my stocking feet. I looked down at my white cotton socks. They were no longer completely white, but they were definitely cleaner than my boots.

I patted the side of my leg for Hawk, leading him over out of the path of anyone else wanting to come into the house via the screen door.

"Down. Stay," I told him, and walked back to the kitchen doorway.

The woman peeked around the door jamb to see Hawk drop to the floor obediently, long forelegs stretched out in front of him. He looked as dignified and imposing as one of the lions at the entrance to the New York Public Library.

"Well, isn't he just something."

She stepped back out of the way to let me in. As I passed her I smelled pungent body odor. But then I reeked of horse, so I figured we were even.

"I'm Judi, Judi with an I," she said as I moved to sit in the straight-backed wooden chair she pointed me to.

"What's your name, hon?"

She was speaking more loudly now, the way people do when they perceive you to be either stupid or foreign-born, apparently confident that increased volume will enhance comprehension.

I paused. "Sandy."

"And your friend outside there?"

Pause. "Hawk. I'm Sandy. He's Hawk."

"And look at us, we both have a bad leg."

She tapped my cane where I had leaned it against the chair.

"That's why I do the cooking, you know. I can't do the fieldwork. Right now I have to get the bread out of the oven."

She pulled on two elbow-length oven mitts and opened first one and then the second oven of the massive old porcelain stove, sliding out baking trays crowded with long crusty loaves.

I saw a covered butter crock sitting on the counter by the refrigerator. My mouth watered as she set the trays on top of the stove to cool.

She took off the mitts and studied me, tilting her head and watching me as I avoided making eye contact. After a few seconds she must have made up her mind.

"I bet you'd like some lemonade, wouldn't you, hon? Nice and cool after working out in that hot sun, with all that dust from the horses."

She bustled around, not waiting for permission, pulling a plastic glass from a cupboard, adding ice, pouring lemonade from a sweating glass pitcher.

She handed me the full glass.

"Now you drink that and you'll be refreshed."

She watched me as I took a sip.

"Isn't that good? So do you need the bathroom, hon? No? Okay then, you just sit right there and I'll go get Finn. And then I have to get this dinner going," she coached herself as she walked quickly and lop-sidedly out of the kitchen the way she had come into it.

I drank the lemonade, the best I have ever had in my life, or ever will have. I wondered if Judi made lemon bars in this kitchen from the zest of the leftover peels of the lemons she squeezed to make the lemonade. If so, I might have to stay on the farm and forget about finding murderers and bringing Loony Rooney to justice.

"Here he is," Judi sang, following Finn into the kitchen.

"I gave Sandy some lemonade," she told him. "She says she's finished her work."

Fin stood in front of where I was sitting and put his hands on his hips to talk to me.

"Come with me now, Sandy. There's someone you need to meet."

He was standing close enough to me, his toes directly in front of mine, that if I stood up we would be almost touching, body to body.

I stayed seated.

"Come along now." He reached out his hand.

I shrank back, turning my shoulder to the side, twisting to the right.

Judi moved to me, standing next to my chair and facing Finn.

"She's just shy, Finn, you can see that, how she's shy with folks. Why don't you let me take her to the goddess for you?"

I think most women can instantly identify who the creepy guys are in the world, and I believe Judi and I were both of the same mind about Finn's palpable creepiness.

Finn stayed where he was. Judi stayed where she was. I looked down at my lemonade glass, my face hidden under the brim of my sun hat.

"All right," he conceded. "Both of you come along then, right now please."

He turned and walked out of the room. Judi sighed with relief. She reached for and took my lemonade glass.

"I bet that lemonade just hit the spot, didn't it

hon?"

Pause. "Yes."

"Come along now, hon. You're going to meet the goddess. She takes care of all of us here, like we're her own children."

I stood and followed her. She took off her apron and hung it up on its hook as we went out. As we walked she checked that her blouse was tucked neatly into her jeans all the way around.

Judi led me out of the kitchen, through a huge white-painted dining hall that had been opened up out of all the smaller rooms on the ground floor of the farm house. There were doors to the outside at each end of the big room. She prattled nonstop as we walked.

"She's our real mother. You're very lucky to meet her. She owns this farm and she gave us all a home when we needed one, and we all have useful work and a community of like-minded people here. And nobody bothers us anymore because the goddess keeps us safe in her embrace of protection and spiritual wholeness."

We reversed direction to climb the painted stairs to the second floor. I think perhaps my blood stopped pumping for a few seconds as we went up. I felt light-headed. I grabbed the banister and planted my cane firmly next to my left foot as I took each step. For a moment I thought I might float up out of my body.

At the upstairs landing we turned and headed down a narrow hallway. I stepped onto a nubbly sisal runner tacked to the wide-plank wood floor and felt through my socks the rough weaving of the rug against the soles of my feet. The old floorboards creaked underfoot as we walked.

I smelled lavender and patchouli and Judi.

Open doors on either side of the hallway allowed light from the house's windows to reach us. I could see twin beds, neatly made, in long rows against the walls of the bedrooms on either side of the hallway.

At the end of the hall Finn stood waiting in the dimness next to a closed door. On the door was a poster of a luminescent full moon rising over the ocean.

A bar of light shone out from under the door onto the dark hallway floor.

I wanted to click my heels together three times and say, "There's no place like home."

I stopped and stood where I was.

"Come along, hon." Judi turned and held out her hand to me. "Nobody's going to hurt you. You're going to meet someone wonderful."

I avoided Judi's hand. I took a step forward, and then another.

I can do this, I reminded myself. *She can't be any more terrifying than my mother.*

I was wrong.

≈20≈

Finn waited until I arrived at the moon-decorated door before reaching across to open it. By reaching across it to turn the doorknob, his body moved in front of mine and almost brushed against my breasts.

Judi had fallen in behind me, and when I lurched backward to avoid Finn I bumped into her. In the ensuing jostling and shifting, Finn grabbed my left arm, ostensibly to steady me.

I tried to yank my arm away from him but he tightened his grip and held on.

I decided that now was not the time to use Krav-Maga on him, although the urge to knee him in the nuts was almost irresistible. I moaned like a whiny child and pulled on my arm instead, as the door in front of us swung open.

"Let her go, Finn."

The voice was a deep resonant contralto. Finn pulled me into the room with a mean squeeze to my arm and then let me go.

I realized with dread that he could very well have shut off my arm phone, or worse, that a recorded message would begin spewing uncontrollably from the sleeve of my dress, announcing to everyone in the room that my call could not be completed as dialed.

Finn shut the door behind us. He walked past me to the far end of the room from where we stood. The upside of his nearness was that he didn't reek the way Judi and I did.

"Praise be, my goddess," said Judi, putting the palms of her hands together as if in prayer. She remained standing behind me at the door.

"Blessings be, my child," the powerful voice responded.

"Your hat. Take off your hat," Judi hissed at me.

I waited, then pulled the faded sun hat off my head and scrunched it in my hands. My clay-caked, sweaty hair fell down my neck in tumbled clumps.

We were in a cool chamber, half the length of

the southeastern end of the big farmhouse. I stood looking at everything peripherally, my face turned away from Finn, Judi, and the Presence I sensed at my far left.

I felt goose-bumps rise on my skin from the sudden transition out of the heat into air twenty degrees cooler than the farmyard and the rest of the house.

Or I could have been a smidgen freaked out.

The room was twenty feet square, with a doorway in the center of the wall at the opposite end of the room from the Presence.

Two loveseats upholstered in aqua shot silk stood between the Presence and Judi and me, flanking a marble-mantled fireplace. Glossy blue and green satin pillows with glittering glass beads at the seams were tucked into the loveseats.

On the coffee table a bowl of pomegranates stood out bright pink-red against the blue.

Beyond the loveseats, in a bay window that curved around behind her, a large woman loomed, sitting on a white, cushioned, throne-like armchair that stretched up at the back almost to the ceiling.

Windows cloaked in light blue velvet were shut against the world at the bay window and on the outer wall of the room. The lightweight sheers behind the curtains floated slightly in the air-conditioned breeze.

A plush spinach-green and bachelor-button blue rug covered most of the gleaming wood floor. The walls were papered in a subtle grass cloth the color of summer squash, with a faint palm leaf pattern imprinted on it.

"Come, child," the voice commanded.

I turned and walked slowly toward the voice, my footsteps silent on the carpet.

Renenet, née Sharonna Rooney, reigning over us mortals from her white throne, was draped in a gossamer pale blue cotton-gauze robe. Wrapped around her head she wore a white turban. On either side of her throne stood tall round pillars, one black and one white.

Oh hell, I thought. *She knows the tarot.*

Because she in her chamber was tricked out essentially as a ringer for the High Priestess. Pillars, pomegranates, palm leaves, pale blue robe, white headdress—it was straight from the Rider/Waite tarot deck design.

Now, there's a reason the tarot images are so compelling and memorable. They represent what Carl Jung dubbed archetypes: universally recognizable representations of human experience and wisdom.

This woman knew that she could command reverence simply by cloaking herself in the trappings of a tarot card's archetypal imagery.

Over the years I've met a number of people

who have told me, "I used to read tarot cards at parties and stuff, and then one time I did a reading that scared the crap out of me and I quit doing it."

And so they should have, the twits. There's something about the cards that guards against frivolous misuse. I'm not smart enough to figure it out.

I do know that the use Sharonna was making of the cards was much worse than frivolous; it was, to me anyway, sacrilegious. To use ancient human knowledge to command falsely the respect and veneration of others is wrong.

If I presume to know the difference between good and evil when I encounter it, I presumed to know that what Sharonna was doing was evil.

So I was angry. I knew I couldn't express my anger. I couldn't get into trouble right now by revealing more than the clueless monotone I had affected would convey.

Hawk was downstairs, my communication link with Thorne was possibly severed, and I was on the second floor of the house with no easy exit in sight. Even had there been an exit, with my still-recovering ankle I couldn't outrun anyone here except maybe Judi.

I also had zero evidence of any criminal wrongdoing, and finding that evidence was the primary reason I had set off on this eminently foolhardy enterprise.

So I seethed silently, and I directed my seething at Finn, who was seated at Sharonna's right on a low white bench. If anyone perceived me to be upset, I hoped I would be perceived as being mad at Finn for touching me.

Which I was, of course, so it was not a challenging anger to feign.

"I am Renenet, my child, goddess incarnate of prosperity and abundance. We are a family here."

She stopped and waited. I think she imagined I might curtsey or bow. I stood straight, with my arms at my sides, looking anywhere but at her or Finn.

"Finn tells me your name is Sandy."

Her low voice was so resonant I felt it not just entering my ears, but moving through the cells in my body.

I said nothing.

"You are good with horses," she said.

I felt drawn to look at her eyes. Her gaze pulled at me, and in my peripheral vision I caught the blackness of her huge irises, glittering like ripe olives in dark brine.

I was genuinely afraid to look at those eyes. I felt like I was in the presence of a gorgon, and that all I had to do was make eye contact and I would be turned to stone.

I also had the feeling that she saw right

through my little performance. I focused on breathing normally and not quaking with fear.

After the sun-bleached browns and grays of the dusty farmyard, and the dimness of the downstairs rooms and upstairs hallway, everything in this chilly, over-furnished, ocean-colored chamber was designed to overwhelm and intimidate—and I was intimidated.

"I brushed Seth and Blossom."

"Finn tells me you tended the horses well."

Pause. "I can fix the harness." I spoke in a monotone. "I need neatsfoot oil and an awl."

I aimed my eyes at the base of the white pillar on Sharonna's left.

"Where did you come from, child?"

I was silent.

She tried taking another tack. "Have you worked on a farm before?"

Pause. "Yes."

"Where was the farm?"

Pause. "Wheatland."

Wheatland is a small farming community halfway to Sacramento, and is far enough away from Marysville that it was unlikely Renenet or Finn would know any of the residents, but not so far away that it was unreasonable for me to have traveled to Marysville from there.

"What did you do on the farm?"

Pause. "I took care of the horses."

"What brought you here, then?"

Pause. "Sold up. Farm got sold up. Horses got sold up. Mr. Jim told me there were farms up north that use horses. You have horses."

Finn shifted on the bench. My sense was that he wanted to mock me, or just interrupt and add his own take on the situation.

Renenet moved her hand subtly in a silencing gesture and he stopped fidgeting.

"How did you come to our farm?"

Pause. "I walked." Pause. "Once in the back of a pickup truck because they didn't like Hawk inside."

Pause. "I asked about horses and a man brought me here."

"How many days did you travel?"

I was silent. Finn couldn't restrain himself.

"She doesn't know. And she doesn't ever say 'no,' either. She just doesn't answer. She won't let anyone touch her. Since Elizabeth is gone we don't have anyone who can drive the horses. This one says they shouldn't rub against each other when they plow, so she must know something about it."

Renenet turned to him and stared silently. He heaved a sigh and was quiet.

I wondered about Elizabeth, and whether she had escaped or been "disappeared."

"Would you like to tend the horses at our

farm?" Renenet asked me.

Pause. "Yes." Pause. "I can fix the harness. Is there an awl? Is there neatsfoot oil?"

"What the hell is an awl?" Finn said, frustration seeping into his voice. "And why does it have to be neatsfoot oil?"

"Be. Still." Sharonna's peremptory tone quieted Finn once more. But she didn't wait for his compliance; she turned her attention across the room to Judi.

"Child, do you have an ice pick in the kitchen?"

"Yes, Goddess."

"After dinner you must loan it to our child Sandy."

"Yes, Goddess."

"And Finn, you will go into town after dinner and obtain neatsfoot oil."

"Why does it have to be that oil specifically?"

"Finn."

Renenet's voice contained no reproach, just command.

We were all silent. Renenet waited to see if there would be more peevishness from Finn and, when there wasn't, she refocused on me.

She decreed her decision with a portentousness that was even more compelling than she had sounded before. I could hear her capitalizing the pronouns as she spoke, assuming divinity.

"You, Sandy, will tend Our horses here. To-night, child, We will welcome you into Our fami-ly."

She raised her forearms, palms up and said, "We are grateful to the beneficent universe for supplying Our need."

"What about the dog?" Finn said. "He's as big as the horses."

Renenet lowered her arms to her lap and pondered.

"You will join Our family," she said to me. "Judi will show you where your bed is to be. Your dog will sleep outside."

I gave it a couple of moments and said, "Hawk is my friend."

"Hawk cannot come inside," Renenet said. "He remains outdoors."

Pause. "I can sleep outside."

"Child, for your safety you must sleep in the sleeping room."

I thought "for your safety" probably meant "so you won't run away when you figure out how hard you have to work to live here."

I stood there silently, saying nothing.

"Goddess, may I speak please?" Judi asked timidly.

"What is it, child?"

"She has that dog really well-trained. He's downstairs on the screen porch now, quiet as a mouse, right where she put him. What if Sandy slept on the screen porch with the dog? This poor child looks like she's slept rough before. I bet the porch would be fine for her. I could tack up an inside latch on the screen door. There's that long wicker settee with the cushions. I could put up one of the folding dividers for privacy. And there's a bathroom downstairs."

Judi had gained momentum as she spoke, finishing in a flourish of enthusiasm for her solution to the conundrum of my dormitory arrangement.

She caught herself.

"Pardon me, Goddess, if I'm speaking out of turn."

Renenet was quiet.

Finn was quiet.

Judi was quiet.

I was quiet.

"If it seems like she's getting special treatment the others will be jealous," Finn said.

Renenet overruled him.

"We will say she is sleeping on the porch because she has to get up earlier than everyone else to tend to the horses. And We made the arrangement out of consideration for the family, because We do not wish for the others to have to tolerate the odor of horses in the sleeping room."

Renenet waited for a moment, I'm guessing to be sure there was no further argument from Finn.

"Child, are you willing to sleep on the porch downstairs? Where your dog is now?"

Pause. "Yes."

Renenet stood, her gauzy robe rustling as she rose to her feet. Standing on the six-inch platform that elevated her throne above the level of the floor, she towered over me.

Finn stood up as well and bowed his head.

Renenet raised her arms in invocation once more and intoned, "Blessings be upon you, Our beloved, Our child, Our protected and guided one. Blessings be upon Our family. Blessings be upon our eternal connection to each other and to the divine which animates us all."

"Blessings be upon you, our Goddess," Finn and Judi responded in unison.

"Come along, then." Finn reached to take my arm.

I stepped away from him, pulling my arms out of his reach.

"You'll get over that fast enough," he leaned in and whispered nastily.

Judi put her arm between us, pushing him firmly away from me.

"Here now, Finn, I'll take her downstairs and she can help me with dinner. Won't you, hon?"

I allowed Judi to herd me out of the room, her arms stretched out on either side of me, sheltering but not touching me.

I was relieved that I had survived the goddess's initial inspection. As we left I heard Finn complaining.

"What are we going to do with that idiot savant? She can't be managed."

As Judi pulled the door shut I heard Renenet's resonant contralto answering.

"We can't farm without the horses, Finn. Clearly they need better care than they're getting since Elizabeth left us. And you have thirty women to choose from. One more that you can't 'manage' won't make any difference."

I wasn't all that worried about the implication that Finn would try to rape me. I could handle that, no problem.

No. What had me horrified right now was the realization that Judi had volunteered me as cook's helper.

≈21≈

"Do you know how to cook, hon?"

Judi was shoving the cooled loaves of bread into a broad basket on top of the refrigerator and setting the baking sheets next to the sink to be washed.

I didn't answer.

"Well, then how about using a peeler? Can you peel the carrots and the potatoes?"

Pause. "Yes."

"Well, that's a big help to me, I'll tell you. I get tired of that chore, I surely do. Here's the pail for the peelings, and here's the pile to get started on."

She pulled down one of the stock pots from its

ceiling hook and filled it halfway with cold water from the sink tap. She set the pot on the butcher block next to me.

"You put the peeled potatoes in the water there so they won't brown in the air. The onions you just need to take off the root and sprout ends and get the paper skin off of them. The carrots you can just set out on the board when they're peeled. Is that clear to you, hon? Do you have any questions? Do you need me to show you?"

I was silent.

"Well, I'll be right here with you anyway to keep an eye on everything," she said.

"Now how about your friend on the porch? Will he eat scraps? Does he need water?"

I put down the peeler and went to the porch without speaking, tucked my crumpled sun hat into the cart, pulled Hawk's dish out of the green plastic bag, and went back to the kitchen to fill the dish for him. I put it down in front of him and Hawk stood up to lap at the cool water.

I turned so my phone arm was away from the kitchen and lifted my sleeve; Finn had indeed managed to disconnect my call to Thorne. I pressed the code for a call.

"I have to feed Hawk," I said, to drown out the sound of Thorne's phone ringing. The ring lasted for almost no time, and I was hopeful Judi, who had been wrangling big pots and pans in the kitchen, hadn't heard it.

I grubbed my way into the kibble bag and pulled out a double handful. Hawk gobbled it all up within a couple of seconds and licked my hands to get the last grainy residue of the food pellets.

"Well, isn't he a good boy," Judi said from the doorway, and I jumped a little and turned toward her.

"Now let's get you washed up so we can get dinner started. I can really use some help in this kitchen, I tell you."

I told Hawk to sit and stay, and went back inside.

In the admittedly small corner of my brain that likes to establish order where there is none, I found pleasure from peeling dozens of potatoes, dozens of carrots, dozens of turnips and parsnips, dozens of sweet onions.

Across from me Judi worked with a cheese grater and a huge chunk of Gruyere, creating mounds of the nutty-smelling cheese on a piece of waxed paper. She hummed to herself and kept an eye on me as I worked.

"You're quick at that, aren't you, hon?"

I scraped the peelings into the pail and watched as, with incredible speed, Judi sliced the vegetables very thin and layered them into two wide baking pans.

She sprinkled grated gruyere between the layers of potato and onion, poured heavy cream over it all, and into the oven they went. She twisted the dial of an old-fashioned white timer and it began to tick.

Judi dressed and seasoned six chickens with fresh rosemary and thyme, stuffing the cavities with leftover squeezed lemons. She loaded the chickens into the other oven to bake while I cut up broccoli and the root vegetables.

Judi pulled out a massive cast-iron frying pan and dropped two big chunks of butter into it. She turned on the burner to start the butter melting.

Suddenly there was a shout from the front yard, followed by a man's voice yelling, "*Christina! Christina, you come right now! Christina! I know you're here!*"

As soon as she heard the man's voice, Judi switched off the burner and moved fast to a button, like an old-fashioned round doorbell buzzer, next to the kitchen light switch.

She pushed the button and a loud bell began to clang, the same one I had heard when Thorne rescued Netta. I covered my ears and limped to Hawk, putting my arms around him and moaning, pretending to be frightened but keeping my eyes open.

The screen door flew back and a petite brunette, panting for breath, jumped onto the porch out of the fading afternoon sunlight. Judi met her at the kitchen door and together they scurried back into the kitchen.

I heard the angry man's voice moving along the side of the house, calling for Christina. He reached the barnyard and kept walking toward the field behind the barn.

I heard the sound of many feet thudding through the barnyard behind me, all of them heading toward the man's voice. I saw the tops of pitchforks and hoes bobbing up and down through the screened windows.

Finn's voice shouted at the man from the second-floor window above the porch—Renenet's window—but I couldn't hear his words. The voices of many women joined the shouting man's and Finn's, everyone shrieking at once in a wild cacophony.

I risked a peek into the kitchen just in time to see Judi shutting the door to a low cupboard in the pantry.

"Now you just shush, hon, not a peep now. He won't find you here," she whispered, and she returned to the kitchen.

She shut both halves of the Dutch door and slid the bolts shut on both halves.

I huddled with Hawk, burying my face against his neck. The noise in the barnyard slowly lessened and stopped.

After a minute or so I heard Finn call out, "That's enough for the day, ladies. You can put the pitchforks away."

I raised myself up enough to peer out through the screens at the far end of the porch. I saw dozens of women walking toward the barn, carrying hoes and pitchforks over their shoulders.

They were talking in normal voices now, but still excitedly. They were hauling something heavy toward the barn. Others were hoeing at the dusty ground, restoring the dustiness.

Opening the door of a lean-to alongside the barn, the rest of the women piled their tools inside. Then they turned around to line up, still chatting and animated, at the barn spigot to wash their hands and faces. Some of them rubbed their clothing under the cold water to rinse out the stains of their recent efforts.

When they were finished scrubbing themselves they shook the water off or dried themselves on the hems of their shirts.

Judi unbolted the Dutch door. I heard Finn's footsteps in the kitchen.

"He's gone," he said to Judi.

"Good riddance to bad rubbish."

Speaking loudly, for my benefit I assumed, she said, "I'm glad I have a new helper, I'll tell you. With everybody coming in to dinner early tonight I wouldn't have been ready without

Sandy's help."

She came to the kitchen door.

"Come on back inside, Sandy. Everything's all right now and we have work to do."

To Finn she said, "We feed a lot of hard workers at mealtimes here, and I like to make them the best food I can. Everything fresh and healthy, the way food should taste. You'll see, Sandy," she added, turning to me.

Finn watched me as I walked with an exaggerated limp to the island and began to shred lettuce into three huge wooden bowls.

I wanted him to think I was more disabled than I actually was. I wasn't sure why; I just did. Using the cane, my gait was essentially normal. But after the long afternoon standing on my feet, it was not difficult to feign a sore ankle.

Finn watched me pick up a head of Romaine and begin shredding it.

"Hunh," he said, and left the kitchen.

Judi went to the pantry and opened the cupboard.

"It's okay now, Christina, honey pie. You can come on out and get washed up. He's gone."

A tiny woman, no more than five feet tall, climbed slowly out of her hiding place and peeked into the kitchen, and then at me.

"That's just Sandy. She's new today."

Judi pointed at me, put a protective arm

around Christina, and walked her to the back door. She stood reassuring the frightened woman.

"Sandy's good with the horses, and she's my new kitchen helper. She's shy, so don't you worry if she doesn't talk to you all that much. And she has a nice dog, a big handsome boy. He's lying right there on the porch as polite as can be, so don't you fret about him if you see him around. Dinner's coming up soon, so you tell everybody to come on inside and set the table, will you, hon?"

I heard the screen door open and shut. Judi came back in and turned the burner back on. She threw cut-up vegetables and garlic into the melted butter to sauté. We went to work finishing the salads.

Two other women, whom Judi introduced as Nancy and Sarah, joined us to help with the rest of the dinner preparation. They shelled peas while we listened to the sounds of women entering the dining room doors from outside. We heard the clatter of silverware as they went about setting the tables. No one mentioned the disturbance in the yard.

"If we had more time I'd make a shortcake, but we don't so it's just going to be fruit for dessert. I hope everybody isn't disappointed in me," Judi said.

From the pantry she brought out baskets of

strawberries from the day's unsold farm stand inventory, and while the peas were parboiling the four of us cut them into four big pottery bowls. We added brown sugar and used our hands to coat the strawberries. The sugar would generate a sweet syrupy juice while we ate the main meal.

At dinner, the goddess and Finn sat at a separate table. The thirty of us women seated ourselves on long benches at mismatched refectory tables. Unspoken but palpable was the residual tension from the afternoon's intrusion.

I shut out what had happened. I don't know how I did that, but I did. I stayed in character, perhaps, living entirely in the moment.

It helped that the food was the best I have ever eaten. I wanted thirds of everything. Until that day I had never eaten, nor wanted to eat, a parsnip. As long as someone as adept as Judi cooked them in the future, I was now on board with the yumminess of parsnips.

I can still taste the strawberries. If only there had been dark chocolate sauce I think I would have asked God to take me right then.

I looked up at one point, savoring the scalloped potatoes, and saw a luminous star pattern painted on the dark blue ceiling. I looked for Orion in the random dots, but he wasn't there.

At the end of the meal Renenet introduced me, announcing to everyone that I would be working with the horses. The women put their hands together as if praying and intoned "Blessings be" at me.

After dinner Judi loaned me an ice pick, so I went back to the barn to fetch the harness straps. I looked around and saw no sign of anything being dragged into the barn earlier. There were hay bales on the floor, but they had been there earlier.

I sat on the porch as evening fell, listening to the women in the kitchen washing dishes while I worked on lengthening the harness straps.

I heard a vehicle coming down the driveway and I looked up to see the big silver pickup truck pulling around and up to the porch.

Finn got out, carrying a paper bag. He brought it to me and put it down on the side table next to my chair. I guessed it was the oil I had asked for, but I wasn't going to open the bag while he was present. I stared at the bag and waited.

He saw that I was working on the harness straps.

"You went into the barn?" There was anxiety in his voice.

Pause. "I'm fixing the harness."

"What did you see? Did you see anything?"

Pause. "I saw two cows and hay and a plow and horse tack."

He studied me for a minute longer.

I sat still and looked at the paper bag.

He made a 'tsk' sound and walked into the house.

I finished lengthening the straps and took Hawk out for a walk, after which I returned the altered straps to the tack room in the barn. Given Finn's concern, I looked around again but I still saw nothing out of place.

There had been a white sedan in the driveway pull-out next to the house when I took the dog out, but it was gone when I got back from our walk.

I came back inside to go to bed on the porch settee.

Judi had brought and unfolded a hinged fabric-covered screen to give me privacy, and had tacked up a hook-and-eye latch on the inside of the screen door. I hooked the door shut.

Through the kitchen doorway I heard the faint sound of footsteps and the murmur of women's voices as they readied themselves to retire for the night.

When I was sure I was at last alone I pulled up my sleeve and said, "Good night" to my arm.

"I'm sorry about earlier," I murmured, "when that jerk grabbed my arm and shut off the phone. Thanks for not sending in the charge of the light brigade. But you heard what's happening here, yes? And we need to talk tomorrow to figure out how to invoke the police."

"Check."

"Did you see it?"

"No. The corral was in the way. But I heard it."

"Okay then. I'll see you in the morning."

"Check," he said. I pushed the button on my bicep to end the call.

I lay down on the cushions in my cotton dress.

I thought that, as tuckered out as I was after the taxing and disturbing day, I would sleep deeply, obliviously, dreamlessly.

Nope.

≈22≈

I awoke from a dead slumber when Hawk touched his cold wet nose to my face.

I pushed his nose away and heard the kitchen door to the porch open. As the porch floorboards creaked from footsteps moving toward us, Hawk growled softly.

The wicker couch squeaked as I first sat up and then stood up in the darkness. There was faint starlight shining in through the mesh porch screens.

Gripping my cane, I took hold of Hawk's collar and we backed away from the divider screen. I looked around me to be sure I knew where the furniture was in case I had to navigate around it or hurl it at someone.

Nothing happened. Then, from the other side of the screen, came a whisper.

"Are you asleep, Sandy? Hon?"

I stopped holding my breath.

I walked back to the screen and folded it shut, leaning it against the wall so I could have a clear pathway out if I needed it.

"There you are," Judi whispered, relieved.

She slumped down into a wooden chair across from the couch where I had been sleeping. She was wearing a loose cotton nightgown and sashed robe. Her feet were bare.

"Can I talk to you for a sec, Sandy? I just need somebody to talk to, and you seem like a good person for that. I don't think you're one to tell tales the way some people do."

I said nothing.

"That's right. You keep mum like that and this'll stay just between us."

I sat on the couch and used a hand sign to get Hawk to sit by my side.

"Wait," I said, and picked up his empty water dish.

"No!" Judi hissed. "Do you have to do that now? They may miss me upstairs."

"Hawk needs water." I kept my voice down.

"Oh, all right. But don't do that in the kitchen,

okay hon? They'll hear you. Go out to the barn."

I was glad to hear her say that.

I slipped on my boots, opened the screen door with exquisite care to be quiet, and padded across the barnyard to the spigot.

As I bent to fill the dish I lifted my dress sleeve and pressed the code for Thorne's phone. The sound of the running water drowned out the ring.

I wiped my feet carefully on the bristly mat as I came back up onto the porch with the full dish. Hawk lapped at the fresh water as soon as I put it down for him.

"He is a good boy, isn't he?" Judi said.

I said nothing. I stared at the unlit lamp next to where she was sitting.

We were quiet for a moment. Judi lifted her face, I'm guessing to listen for any noise from the house above her. Satisfied, she reached across to take my hand, and when I shrank away from her, apologized.

"I'm sorry hon. I forgot. It's just that I'm used to being close when I talk to my girlfriends. I miss that. You can't be close like that here. I was close with Elizabeth and now she's gone and there's nobody I can be close with anymore."

She shook her head. I said nothing.

"I want somebody to hear this. I want to have said something about what goes on here, in case something happens to me. Do you see, hon?"

I said nothing. I looked at the lamp.

"I stepped on the sides of the stair steps so they wouldn't make a noise when I came down, so it would be safe. Most of us, you see, we came here because we needed to find a safe place.

"We all of us women just want to be safe, you know? Mostly from men, I'm sorry to say. Why we can't raise up our men to be better men I can't say, but we can't, I guess. Most of us here got away by the skin of our teeth. We were all just a hair away from being beaten to death."

Judi put her hand on her knee.

"That's what happened to my leg. My husband kicked me so hard he broke my kneecap, and it never did heal up right. While I was in the emergency room a nurse came to me and saw the bruises on me everywhere and she talked to me and talked to me and finally I got some sense in my head and she brought in some women who helped me to sneak away and disappear."

Judi patted her hand up and down on her knee.

"I knew my husband would track me down and find me no matter where I went, and I went to a lot of places to get away, and he found me more than once at the shelters and made trouble. He made so much trouble that they had to call the police to make him leave. I had to move around from shelter to shelter, and it was so hard. I was lucky not to have any kids, I guess. The women at the shelters who had kids were really stuck."

I wanted to interrupt her. I wanted to say that it's not just men we are raising up incorrectly if women are allowing themselves to be beaten more than once by the same person. Men and women both are complicit if there is ongoing violence that is not part of a consenting-adult whips-and-chains relationship.

In San Francisco, where there are Mom & Pop bondage equipment stores all over town, there must be plenty of customers who enjoy inflicting damage without actually killing each other, or else the places couldn't stay in business for very long. Their customers want to wear a ton of metal-studded leather that requires complicated lacing, and any damage inflicted is accompanied by pleasure.

I don't personally get it, but I don't have to.

Judi shook her head sadly. I refocused on her.

"I was waiting for a bus to Louisville. I was heading back home where my people are from, when Finn walked up and spoke to me and told me about this place.

"I think it was because I was on crutches, you know? From my broken knee? I think he picks up on the ones who look like they're weak. He takes the cars that the men who come here leave behind and drives down to Sacramento and Stockton and Merced and sometimes even to San Francisco, to the parks and the bus stations, and he finds women like me and we all come up here to escape."

Judi looked up at the ceiling, considering what to say next.

"For some reason I believed him, that this farm was where women could go and work and be part of a family and never be found by their husbands or boyfriends or even the police. I just wanted to disappear, you know? And I believed what Finn told me, like I was hypnotized or something, and here I am. I've disappeared. And I'm safe."

She paused. "Maybe," she added.

She was silent.

I was silent. I stared at the lamp.

"But I haven't disappeared altogether, like some people," she whispered, putting her finger to her lips.

"This is the hard part to say, because this family protects itself. Renenet understands us all because her father beat her mother—she told us so. That's why she created this 'haven,' she calls it. And it's not like the men who come around don't mean us harm. They do. They do mean us harm. You saw that today, didn't you, hon? With Christina?"

Pause. "Yes," I whispered.

"She's such an itty-bitty thing, and that husband of hers was a big brute to her. But tomorrow morning early, before the sun comes up, if you're awake real early, you're going to see some of the women outside working before breakfast, over beyond the horse corral, and I want you to stay away. Do you understand, hon? I want you to stay away."

Pause. "Stay away."

"Yes, hon, you have to stay away. I'm not sure how to say this, but there are some of the women here who don't agree with how Finn and Renenet take care of us when trouble comes, but they don't dare say anything. And what happens here from time to time isn't for everyone to see. It's secret, you know?

"And some of them, like Elizabeth? She didn't come here because her husband beat up on her. She was just homeless and had nowhere else to go. She was a widow, and she still loved her husband, the way some of us others do, even the ones like me whose husbands were so mean to them.

"I don't know how that can be, but people are strange. I will say that there are times I miss my husband, I truly do, if I'm honest. But if he came here and found me, he'd kill me, I know he would."

"There aren't any kids here," I said, before I could catch myself.

But Judi seemed not to notice that I had offered up information out of character.

"No, no kids." She shook her head sadly.

"That's the other thing Elizabeth couldn't abide. If anyone ever gets pregnant Renenet says it's a sin against the family, and that we can't raise children here because it would bring the outside world into the farm, with vaccinations and schools and all that public notice that could be dangerous to us.

"She says we're all her children and we're each other's family. But Finn has relations with some of the women, I know he does. They sneak out together in the night time. I hear them go out the back way to the barn. If they get pregnant from it Finn gives them a pill."

She thought for a moment.

"He brought back this sweet young girl a month or so ago, such a nice child, but younger than the rest of us. He kept a special eye out for her, hon, all the time. You could see him watching her wherever she went, but I know she didn't like him. When she wouldn't go along with him he put her to work out in the field, even though you could see she wasn't raised to do that kind of work.

"That Netta, her name was Netta, she was

smart. She helped me so much in the kitchen at first. She told me her Momma was a good cook, and she was a big help to me because she'd learned so much from her Momma. That child confided in me. I don't know why people confide in me, but they do. We're in the kitchen and we're cooking and they get to telling me their stories.

"Netta let on that she was in trouble when she came up here. She said she'd had a fight with her Momma about it and she was afraid of what her Daddy would do. She was just a child, and I can't believe her parents wouldn't have forgiven her and taken her back. But she wouldn't believe me when I told her that. Maybe she knew better than I did what her parents would do to her. She said she was scared of them, and then she got the morning sickness and Finn gave her a pill and she wasn't in trouble no more."

Judi paused and thought.

"A few weeks later some people came and dragged her out of the field so fast nobody could stop them. It was awful. And now I'll never know what became of that child."

Judi sighed and stood up.

"So I understand why Finn and the goddess have the rules they do. They have to keep the family safe. They take care of us and we work hard for each other. We care about each other, and we have a good life here. Now and again it would be a true pleasure to soak in a nice hot bubble bath, but that's not as important to me as it used to be. What's most important is that we're safe here.

"Elizabeth was going to tell people how we stay safe. Finn and Renenet and the family took care of Elizabeth when she had nowhere else to go and she said she didn't care. She was going to tell outsiders about how we protect ourselves. She confided in me that she was going to, and I believed her. I never tattled on her about that, but somebody must have."

Judi turned to go, and then turned back and sat down again.

"There are times I wonder who I am now, you know, hon? So here I am talking to you because I want somebody to know me, the real me. I want to have confided in somebody, but I want to be safe at the same time. I don't want to be somebody who hasn't told the truth about the things that happen on this farm. But I understand why us women have to be safe. I feel the puzzlement of it all in my heart."

I said nothing.

I thought of the Four of Cups card, of discontent with what has happened, and the anticipation of discontent with what might happen.

"Thank you for listening to me, hon," she whispered, and tiptoed to the kitchen door.

"You remember now, Sandy, stay away in the morning."

"Stay away," I said.

"Good girl. Thanks for hearing me out. Nighty night, and don't let the bedbugs bite."

Judi shut the kitchen door behind her.

I took Hawk out with me outside, all the way behind the barn to where I was sure I wouldn't be overheard.

"I don't think this can wait until tomorrow," I said to my arm.

"Check."

"Isn't it time for the police?"

"Yes."

"Who has the job of calling them? I think I do, yes? Because the police have to be aware of the almost entirely female population here, and Renenet probably contributes to local police charities in order to be left alone.

"I'm guessing people are sympathetic to the women here. If a man calls the police, I'm thinking the response won't be as prompt as it would be if a woman called. And until the crew of women starts to work, I won't know exactly where the body is."

"Yes."

"Are we synchronizing watches? Because I don't know what time 'before breakfast' is, and I don't have a watch. They'll go out the side doors of the dining room and I may not hear them."

"Can you stay awake?"

"Maybe. Probably. What time is it?"

"Two-thirty. I'll call you at five and head over closer to keep watch."

"Okay."

So we had a plan. It wasn't much of a plan, given the circumstances.

I was going to have to wait. Waiting is not widely acknowledged to be one of my superior talents. Meddling, sure, but remarkably few people would single out 'waiting' as a skill that comes naturally to me.

There was no way around it, though; I was going to be stuck with biding some time.

I shut off the panther phone and went back into the house to do the necessary biding.

And met Finn.

So I didn't have to wait after all.

≈23≈

"Hi there, Sandy."

He was sitting in a chair next to the porch screen door, barefoot, wearing a white T-shirt and jeans. He stood up and grabbed my left arm as soon as I pulled the door outward.

I whined and pulled at my arm to break free. Hawk was outside behind me, growling, trying to shove past me through the narrow doorway, trying to get at Finn.

"Who were you talking to? You can stop the dummy act. We heard you talking to someone even if we couldn't see him."

I stopped straining to get my arm loose. I

could feel the phone overlay, including its tiny root into my bloodstream, being yanked out of my tattoo, and then I felt blood leaking from the incision.

"Hawk!" I said. "Off!"

Hawk stood still and was quiet.

"We have to talk to Renenet. Tell the dog to stay here."

"Let go of me," I said, looking him in the eye, "and I will."

Finn, no doubt startled by my direct eye contact, let go of my arm. I felt the phone decal flutter off like soot-colored ash and waft to the floor. In the dark, Finn missed it.

I told Hawk to stay outside and I shut the screen door between us.

I wasn't afraid of Finn. I wanted to talk to Renenet, for my mother's sake, for my own sake.

I wanted to ask about Phil, who went up in flames in his Mustang, and whose death and its aftermath wrecked my mother.

"I won't walk up the stairs in front of you," I said. "You go first or I'm not going."

I wouldn't put it past him to engage in a little skirt lifting if I were in front of him. His grin was bright in the darkness.

"There are a lot of women here who like what I can do for them."

Well, that was the limit for me. I reached a

hand up as if to caress his cheek, braced my knees, and with my other fist I socked him as hard as I could in the nuts.

He made an involuntary noise, and bent and grabbed his crotch with both hands.

I used my knuckles to hit him straight on in his unguarded throat, just above the Adam's apple.

With the thick heel of my boot I stomped as hard as I could on his instep and heard a quiet but satisfying pop.

Finn crumpled to the floor and curled up into a fetal position, his breathing ragged and rasping.

Good. I didn't want him asphyxiated, just immobilized.

"Find Thorne," I commanded Hawk, and pointed at the neighboring farm. He lifted his nose and stood still for a moment, and then took off like a raven-black bullet train across the barnyard.

I went into the house. I kept my boots on, tiptoeing on the edges of the stairs as Judi had suggested, and I was mostly silent as I passed the dormitories full of slow-breathing women on either side of the hallway to Renenet's room.

I opened the moon-decorated door and walked in. There were candles in hurricane lamps on the fireplace mantle. I smelled beeswax and lavender and frankincense.

The High Priestess was not ensconced on her throne.

I opened the door on the right and there she was, tucked cozily into a king-size four-poster canopy bed with pale blue drapes hanging from the top rails. She was reading a book. Her black hair hung loose around her shoulders, thick and curved into coils that glinted like lumps of coal.

"Hello, Sharonna."

"I thought you might come up and pay me a visit."

She tucked her index finger into the page to hold her place.

"Finn told me Judi was downstairs having a chat with you. You'd think by now everyone would have figured out that there are micro-phones everywhere. But no, they all think I'm omniscient." She picked up a bookmark on the nightstand and slipped it into the book where her finger had been. She put the book down next to the nightstand's hurricane lamp.

"Well, I suppose Finn was right about you. I suppose I was right about you, too. Even wearing that ridiculous hat and decked out like a bag lady you are the spitting image of your mother."

She made eye contact with me at last, and I felt a jolt of unease. Her eyes were black and lu-minous and the way she spat out "your mother" was venomous.

"She told me you killed Phil," I said, working to keep a quaver out of my voice, "and you threatened to say her father had slept with you if she told anyone she suspected you."

"And?"

"And?! Christ, Sharonna! Why murder Phil? Why threaten a scandal for my mother's family?"

"Because they deserved it, dear. Your mother and her little clique made my life an utter misery. And then Louisa fixed me up with her cousin, and he and I were lovers for a few weeks, and it was the only time in my entire young life that I was truly happy.

"But then I found out I was pregnant, and I told Phil, and of course he tried to dump me. I could hear it in his voice that he was going to do it as soon as he called me to ask me to go up to Marin that night. When we got there he told me he'd fallen in love with your mother. He was a swine, like all the rest of them."

"You thought he deserved to die for that? You were teenagers!"

"Yes. We were teenagers."

Sharonna spoke matter-of-factly, clasping her hands together on the cotton coverlet and glaring at me with her magnetic dark eyes. Against her pale skin the dark eyes and hair were dramatic and transfixing.

I made myself blink and broke the spell.

She went on.

"I told him we could still see each other while he dated your mother, but he wouldn't hear of it. Anyway, I had stolen a bottle of my father's vodka and I beaned Phil with it when he wouldn't even look me in the eye. And then I poured the vodka all over him and that damned car he was so proud of, where he used to fuck me in the back seat, and I lit him up with the cigarette lighter."

She spoke the words without a trace of regret.

"When my parents found out I was pregnant they hustled me off to a home for unwed mothers, if you can believe such things ever existed, and I spent seven long months there until I had the baby, and then something went wrong during the birth and that was it for me. No more children."

"And Finn is your son?"

"Yes. Named for his father, of course. Finneran Rooney after Philip Finneran. If I couldn't give him a last name I could at least give him a first name. I made the adoption agreement include a guarantee that he could keep his first name.

"I found him when they unsealed the records a few years ago. He'd been looking for me as well, and he dropped out of school and moved up here to be with me."

She paused for a moment and then spoke even more coldly than before.

"He resembles Phil very much. And he behaves exactly like his father and grandfather with the women here. Except when he's with me, Finn behaves like an oversexed martinet. He likes believing he's in charge of all these women."

"How did you wind up at this farm?"

"It was my grandfather's. He left it to my mother and I was the only one who wanted it. My grandfather loved me, I know he did. He was the only man who ever did. I learned from my father and Phil and every other man that men are all tyrants. They think they deserve to rule the world.

"But all the power they've usurped from women is coming back to us now. I'm in the vanguard. And I won't let anything prevent me from keeping this farm and protecting the women who come here for seclusion and protection."

I was horrified. I hear women mock and dismiss men as a gender and vice versa and I don't understand it. We are humans, and we share this earth, and it seems to me that amity and understanding are always preferable to enmity and disdain.

This vindictive woman was not protecting anyone but herself, and she kept a vanguard of subjugated women in front of her as a shield, lured to her by her misbegotten son.

I'd had enough of Finn, and now I'd had more than enough of her.

"You work them like drones. You don't let them bathe or have any privacy. You kill their husbands and brothers and fathers and sons and pregnancies. You can't keep the secret any longer of what happens here. I'm not the only one who knows what's going on. Netta knows, her father knows, and I'm betting the people in town know. You're finished, Sharonna."

I was trying to talk sense to her. It was like trying to talk sense to a wind-driven forest fire, but I tried anyway.

Her face reddened and she sat up in the bed. I'm guessing the goddess wasn't used to being argued with. Watching her color rise, I grasped at the weak hope that she would become so apoplectic that she would keel over from a stroke.

But no. She used her magnificent resonant voice.

"The women here *are* drones, working for the benefit of the community. And no one will find out Our secrets if I forbid it. And I do forbid it. I shall not be gainsaid. My wrath is just and unmerciful."

She turned to the side of the bed and lowered her feet to the floor. She reached behind her, under the pillow, and out came a pistol.

Facing me, she held the gun at her side for the time being. She frowned, and sighed with impatience.

"Come along now, Sandy, if that's really your name. We're going to take a little walk outside."

I heard footsteps thumping across the barn-yard, and then Hawk's sharp bark. Sharonna and I exchanged a look and then she pointed the gun at my chest.

I heard a ripping sound and felt through the floor the slap of the screen door below us. I realized that Hawk had dived through the screen door's mesh without waiting for the door to be pushed open.

Sharonna and I stared at each other, immobilized, as we heard the dog's claws scrabbling on the dining hall floor downstairs and then on the wooden steps of the stairway as he bounded up to find me for Thorne.

Hawk was flying. My monster doggy was in full charge, anticipating a big biscuit.

The sound of the one-hundred-twenty-pound animal slamming against the door to her room, baying like a Peterbilt truck horn, pulled Sharon-na's glance away for a moment. With all my might I swung the curved end of my cane at the hand holding the pistol.

The gun flew out of her hand, thumped against the wall, and fell down to the carpeted floor, ten feet away from us both.

She grabbed her smacked hand and cradled it, looking at the pistol where it lay, and I suppose gauging whether she could beat me to it.

I think she forgot that I was gimpy, or maybe she thought my cane was merely another prop in my act. I stood there debating whether to lunge and jab her in the solar plexus, leap for the gun myself, or bonk her on the head with my cane if she went for the gun.

Sharonna was thinking, and then she made up her mind. She turned, grabbed the hurricane lamp from the nightstand, and dashed to the closet on the wall behind her. She yanked open the door and disappeared inside.

I heard Thorne's boots on the stairs, and the cries of the women in the dormitories.

The alarm bell began to clang.

I didn't bother worrying about why Sharonna ran to her closet. I retrieved the gun just as the bedroom door burst open.

I held out my arms to hug Thorne and hug my lovely, humongous search-and-destroy doggy. First-come, first-served on the hugs, but Hawk did his best to dominate everything.

We were so happy to be together that we momentarily forgot about what tended to tran-spire when the alarm bell rang.

Thorne is indeed stupefyingly puissant, but I doubt anyone would refuse to accept that thirty angry women acting in concert, even wearing nighties and slippers, are downright invincible.

≈24≈

Thorne remembered first.

I know this because he said, "Oh shit," and ran to slam the chamber door shut. He shot the metal bolt across into its round slot.

"There are thirty of them," I said. "They'll break down the door. And where was Finn when you came in? I left him on the porch floor."

"Stomped him."

Well, okay.

There was pounding and shouting at the chamber door. Someone kicked at the doorknob and the door shuddered. I remembered the closet and pointed.

"This way."

I took hold of Hawk's collar and handed the gun over to Thorne.

We all stood to the side as he slowly pushed open the closet door. Thorne unclipped a flashlight from his belt and shone it around to see inside.

On one wall was a clothing rod full of pale blue garments, and above that stretched a horizontal rack on which was an array of white headdresses on Styrofoam forms. Below the garments sat a neatly paired row of shoes. One pair was missing from the row.

There was a miniature door on the rear wall of the closet.

"Really?" I said. "Are there little cookies we're supposed to eat first?"

The outer door to Sharonna's chamber splintered. Someone had found an axe.

"Go," Thorne said, and pushed the dog and me into the closet. Thorne pulled the closet door shut behind him and aimed the flashlight at the little door on the opposite wall.

Once again we stood to the side, this time brushing against the blue robes and engulfing ourselves in the scent of lavender.

We listened. All we heard was the sound of the axe breaking down the chamber door and the shouts of encouragement from the women.

Thorne pushed the pint-sized door open. It

was dark behind it, and impossible to see what was back there. He leaned down to point the flashlight into the darkness.

"Stairs," he said, and got down on all fours to crawl through the doorway.

I waited until he gave me the go-ahead by knocking twice with the flashlight on the metal of the spiral staircase before sending Hawk down.

Hawk had difficulty navigating the tight spiral curve of the stairs. He vacillated and had to be coaxed. When the dog neared the bottom Thorne held out his arms and Hawk jumped into them.

If they weren't both so Brobdingnagian it would have been precious.

I scooted down the stairs on my butt, hooking my cane around the upright newels to anchor myself and keep from tumbling.

At the bottom of the stairway was another mini-door. We were jammed together in the semi-darkness, between the bottom step and the door. I heard footsteps and shouting from above us, but so far no one followed us into the emergency exit at the back of Sharonna's closet.

Thorne turned off the flashlight and tried to push open the door. It wouldn't budge. He took out his do-everything gadget and flipped open a knife blade, sliding the blade upward along the unhinged side of the door, where the latch would be.

I heard a click and the door opened outward. We were in the pantry, in the cupboard where Judi had tucked Christina yesterday afternoon.

Thorne handed me his phone and said, "Nine-one-one."

He ducked and hauled himself forward by his arms out of the cupboard.

I heard the 911 operator's greeting and told her where I was and what had happened, and that there were injuries and to send help in a hurry. I made myself sound slightly hysterical.

Well, maybe I *was* slightly hysterical. An axe-wielding mob was hunting me.

The operator wanted me to stay on the line, but I didn't. I hunkered down and crawled out into the pantry next to Thorne, handing him the phone, which began to ring. Nine-one-one was calling back.

Thorne pressed Stop on the phone and then removed the battery, tucking everything into his shirt pocket and buttoning the pocket shut.

"We don't know where the body is," I said.

"Sharonna and Finn."

"Ah, of course. They'll know we're calling in the law. They're disposing of the evidence."

I heard sirens in the distance.

"We have to stop them," I said.

"We do."

Thorne handed me the gun. He pointed at the

safety, showed me how to undo it, and I suddenly wished I had agreed to learn how to shoot something more lethal than nice photographs with my smart phone.

We went out onto the porch.

No Finn.

Beyond the horse corral a faint glow drew our attention.

"She took a hurricane lamp with her," I whispered.

I followed Thorne as he strode across the barnyard. You'd think he'd have made noise in his work boots, but he didn't. He's a stealthy juggernaut when he wants to be. I had Hawk by the collar and my boots scuffed along in the barnyard dirt.

We stopped at the horse corral. I used hand signs to tell Hawk to sit and stay. He was still excited, and probably feeling betrayed that there had been no biscuit waiting for him when he found Xana like a good doggy, but he sat down anyway.

In the dim light we saw Sharonna and Finn dragging something unwieldy toward the manure pile. She urged him to hurry.

Seth and Blossom ambled over, blowing bursts of air out of their nostrils and nickering quietly, to see if there were any carrots in my pockets. I was a massive letdown on all the four-legged fronts.

The sirens were louder now, a half a mile or so away. The strobe of their roof-rack flashers bounced off the white paint of the big farmhouse. I could sense Thorne's unease at the prospect of many policemen descending on us.

"Thorne, I've got this, okay? You can go."

"No."

I realized what it took for him to stand with me then. I knew he was acutely aware that the on-the-grid world was seconds away from swooping in and snatching him up in their "show-me-some-I.D." talons.

I stepped up onto the lowest rung of the corral fence and aimed the pistol at the sixty-foot long manure pile, about twenty feet to the right of where mother and son were heading. The tarp-covered mound wasn't precisely the broad side of a barn, but I was pretty sure I could hit it.

I flipped off the safety, held the gun in both hands, aimed, and fired.

The sound reverberated through the night. Sharonna and Finn looked up in shock. The horses wheeled and galloped to the far side of the corral.

I fired again.

Finn dropped his half of the burden, picked up the hurricane lamp and ran to the barn, his gait uneven on his damaged foot.

Sharonna shrieked, "Finn!" and ran after him, her pale blue nightgown stained at the bottom from what they had been doing, and where.

She caught up to her son as he was pulling open the barn door and they struggled. She was bigger and stronger than he was.

I knew Finn was hurt from when I hit him earlier, but anyway Sharonna held him fast during the struggle.

Finn lost his grip on the hurricane lantern to battle her and the glass fell and shattered. The candle flame caught the straw on the barn floor, but in their struggle neither mother nor son noticed.

Sharonna's nightgown lit up at the hem and wisps of flame wafted up around her. She pulled Finn into the barn with her and shut the door.

I yelled, *"Fire!"* as three police cars skidded into the barnyard. From the farmhouse streamed dozens of screaming, nightgown- and pajama-clad women.

Judi and another woman were brave enough to run into the barn and drag out the two bellowing milk cows. The women staggered back out coughing, but were otherwise okay, and the cows were saved.

I tried to stop Thorne from going in to retrieve Sharonna and Finn, but he went after them anyway when he saw Judi go in for the cows.

I was frantic, and even worse at waiting than usual, until he finally stumbled out empty-handed, choking and weeping from the smoke. I could smell burning hair when he staggered over to me. He leaned on the corral, gasping for breath.

A burning barn is a godawful dreadful thing to watch, but, like any fire, you can hardly take your eyes off it.

I opened the corral gate and pulled the skittish draft horses away to the front of the house so they wouldn't panic and do damage to themselves or anyone else. I wound up tying them to the railing of the front steps after sending Thorne through the house to fetch my cart and the blue nylon rope.

I carried feed and water from the corral to the horses and sat with them and with Hawk, away from everyone else.

No one had seen Thorne charge into the house with Hawk earlier. They had heard him but the house had been dark, so when they saw him in the barnyard in the midst of the chaos I'm guessing they thought he had run over from a nearby farm to help, the way neighbors do in a crisis.

But now he was nowhere to be found. I assumed he had returned to the adjacent farm to strike camp.

The firefighters worked fast to connect their hoses and aim water at the barn, but it was a futile effort. The hay and the wooden structure had gone up very fast. They could do little but soak the remaining rubble.

I limped to the back of the house and found the police officer in charge, standing there like everybody else, mesmerized by the sight of the fire.

"Have you done a headcount?" I asked.

"Yes. We're missing a man and a woman."

"They're in the barn. I saw them start the fire. They dropped a burning lantern."

"What's your name, Miss? Who did you see drop the lantern?"

"Sharonna Rooney and her son Finneran are in there. But first I need to show you something, sir. Please. It can't wait. They murdered a man."

I led him to the manure pile and he used his flashlight to see what was there. He called to another officer and they began organizing around the mangled body. I backed away as they concentrated their attention on cordoning off the area. I did not envy them the search that they, or more likely some lowlier cop, would have to make for other bodies.

If the police officer wanted to talk to me again, I hoped there was enough confusion going on that he would think I was just another member of the crowd of distraught women, and he could talk to me later when the fire was out.

No one knew I was a fake; everyone still thought of me as Sandy. Except for the cop everybody thought I was mentally disabled, so none of the women bothered with me. I went back to the front of the farmhouse and sat with the horses.

At one point I looked up at the night sky and saw Orion directly overhead. I believe that gratitude, no matter how seemingly pointless, is never in vain.

"Thank you," I said to the stars, light-years away from me.

As dawn began to fade the blue-black sky to periwinkle, Thorne pulled the Chrysler up to the farm stand.

I said goodbye to the horses, told Hawk to heel, grabbed my cane and cart, and walked slowly and carefully out the driveway past the fire trucks to the car.

I pulled bath towels from the trunk to wrap around me, shielding the leather seats from my *eau-de-chevaux* stench.

From my wheely-cart Thorne spread Hawk's dog blanket across the back seat and the dog hopped in cheerfully and lay down. He heaved a sigh, shut his eyes and slept.

Thorne backed the car around carefully, came to a full stop at the edge of the highway, looked both ways, put on the blinker, turned slowly, and drove us all the way home.

I know he did, because when I woke up we were parked in the dark in our garage, the engine was ticking as it cooled, and he was holding my hand.

Upstairs, I climbed into the shower to scrub away the vestiges of my lately untranquil mind.

⪧25⪦

I was sitting in the shade of the awning on the patio behind DeLeon's house. The afternoon sun had heated the backyard to what I considered a scorching temperature—the Oakland hills get much hotter than cool, foggy San Francisco. From where I was sitting I could see all the way to the Golden Gate Bridge.

I was wearing a sleeveless linen blouse and cutoffs. A sheer bandage was taped to my arm, where the little phone incision was healing. I had scrubbed off all but the ghost of the panther tattoo after getting back to San Francisco from Marysville.

A sweating glass of iced tea sat on the little table next to my chair. A few feet away, out in the sun but wearing a Tulsa University ball cap and wraparound sunglasses against the glare, DeLeon stood basting ribs on the barbecue.

He laughed at something Maxine whispered to him, reaching his arm around her waist as she set down a tray of marinated onions for her husband to grill.

I had my recuperating ankle up on a little ottoman that Netta had brought outside for me. I was off the cane at last, wearing a running shoe and socks with a compression bandage inside to hold my ankle together so it wouldn't swell up much if I was on it all day.

It was hot enough that I took off my shoes and tucked my rolled-up socks into them. I poked my bare feet out of the shade into the sun and wiggled my once-again pedicured toes. The heat felt nice.

I heard Terrell say something to one of his friends. They were inside, watching a baseball game on TV.

"I invited Mater," DeLeon said to me after Maxine headed back inside for more food.

"Get out."

"I'm serious."

"What did she say?"

"She was honored by the invitation, and regretted to say she was otherwise engaged."

"Did you tell her the right day?"

"Maybe I did and maybe I didn't."

We laughed.

"Some horses are too high for Mater to climb down off of," I said. "Or, wait a moment. According to her rules, I'm not supposed to end a sentence with a preposition. Down off of which it is too high for Mater to climb."

"She said 'thank you for everythin' to me."

"Really?"

"She said I was the reason you found that devil woman. She said it was justice for Loony Rooney to burn in a fire."

"Oh, DeLeon, I don't know if I feel like there was any justice. I don't know that anyone deserves to burn for what they do in this life. We're all wounded creatures, and some wounds heal and some never do. No matter how hard we try, we can act wrong because the scarring left from those wounds binds us into behavior we know is wrong."

"Miz Xana, you know and I know that it's for all of us to learn how to stay right in spite of the scars."

"Yes. I do know that. If we're in touch with our genuine selves we know the right thing to do and that we ought to find the strength to do it. But I can still feel sorrow for those who can't manage to listen to their better angels."

"Well, you have a more forgivin' heart than I do, is what I will say to you about that."

We were quiet. I sipped my iced tea and he took a swig of beer from the bottle he had resting in the shade of the barbecue.

"Do you know what happened to the farm and the women?" he asked me.

"I went back up there and talked to the woman who confided in me about what had been happening there. She was a little discombobulated at seeing me the way I really am, but she's a soft-hearted soul and she forgave me for the trick I played on her.

"Sharonna, believe it or not, had created a trust, and two of the women were named trustees, so they took over and are running the farm now. One trustee was this woman I spoke to named Judi, and I think she'll get the place straightened out pretty well.

"I gave her a book on the proper care of draft horses, and another one on farming with them. I bought her a new horse brush, too, and a big bag of mini-carrots.

"She told me there was insurance, so the barn's going to get rebuilt. The police found a total of six bodies, and they attributed them all to Sharonna and her son. I'm not about to tell them otherwise, because the men were abusers and the women were defending themselves. There's no forensic evidence to prove any of the women were involved because all the wooden farm tools went up in flames during the fire and the metal parts melted out of shape. I know some people will think I'm wrong about letting the blame fall entirely on Finn and Sharonna, but that's too bad."

"What if one of the ex-husbands shows up tryin' to make trouble?"

"Judi's arranging to hook up an alarm that goes straight to the police station in Marysville, and that anyone can activate from anywhere on the farm. The women are working on getting restraining orders put in place and they're going to let the police handle intruders from now on."

"I saw on the news they found the bitch goddess and her son in the barn."

"Yes. They found Sharonna and Finn once the fire was finally extinguished. Apparently there was a room under the barn floor, just like Thorne predicted, and that's where they temporarily hid the bodies of the men who came looking for the women. They shoved hay bales over the entrance so outsiders wouldn't find it. We're guessing Sharonna and Finn went in there to hide from the police, but the fire got them.

"Sometimes a woman would hide in there too if a man came looking for her and the woman was too far out in the field to make it back to the farmhouse cupboard. If ever there was a man's body put into the cellar room during the day, before breakfast the next day a crew of women would sneak out to bury the body in the compost, After a good long while they would use the compost to grow their very special organic vegetables."

DeLeon studied the onions Maxine had brought him to cook.

"I think that's enough of that topic, don't you?" I said. "How's Netta doing? She looks much better."

Netta was floating on her back in the swimming pool.

"My baby girl is much, much better, thanks to you and your man."

He spoke quietly, glancing at her to see if she could overhear.

"She's been seein' the shrink, goin' to summer school to make up for the time she lost. She broke up with that boyfriend."

DeLeon stared at his daughter, then back at the grill. He spoke softly, with a catch in his voice.

"There is no way to ever repay you for what you and Thorne have done for my child. For my whole family."

With a big brush DeLeon dabbed sauce on the ribs and scrutinized his handiwork. He sniffed and rubbed a knuckle across his nostrils.

"You don't understand," I said. "I did it for my family as well as yours. We're even. Or maybe, now that I think about it, I still owe you."

"How can that ever be?"

I could see DeLeon's eyes looking at me through his dark glasses.

"My mother told me she loved me. And I found out why, or at least partly why, she is the way she is. I can forgive her now. Or maybe I can forgive myself for thinking I was never going to be who or what she could love. What anyone could love."

Behind my own sunglasses I was tearing up a little.

Thorne ducked his head under the top edge of the sliding glass door and stepped out onto the patio. His blond hair, shorn into slightly less of a mop in order to remove the scorched areas, lit up in the sun like a torch. He smiled his eentsy smile at me, and I smiled my wider smile back.

He strolled over and sat on the chair next to me—the chair on the sunnier side—so his bulk could afford me more shade.

He lifted his feet to put them on the ottoman, and I lifted my bare feet in perfect synchrony and let them rest on top of his crossed legs.

"Babe," he said.

Bevan Atkinson, author of *The Tarot Mysteries* including *The Fool Card*, *The Magician Card*, *The High Priestess Card*, and *The Empress Card*, lives in the San Francisco Bay Area and is a long-time tarot card reader.

Bevan currently has no pets but will always miss Sweetface, the best, smartest, funniest dog who ever lived, although not everyone agrees with Bevan about that.